Insane

By
Anita Giannantonio

Contents

Chapter One

Present Day

It was one of the first chilly days of fall. The warmth of summer had lasted longer than usual, the budding flowers and green leaves only just starting to show hints of yellows and oranges, seemingly oblivious to the death that lurked in the shadows, patiently biding its time before flipping the switch and casting the rural countryside of central Pennsylvania into a swath of lifeless gray for the next six months. The town of Pennsdale sat nestled in farmland and had the habit of being particularly hard hit by the winters. Most of the locals had spent that Saturday doing last-minute tidying up and preparations for the cold that would soon follow.

Josh Mabry was busy cutting firewood, which he stacked neatly to the side of his home under the cover of a shed. He wore a plaid button-down shirt, work pants, and thick gloves to prevent him from having to dig out splinters later. He had put off the chore for months and had reluctantly agreed to finish the woodpile at his wife's nagging. The sun had just set, and dinner was almost ready. The smell of pot roast wafted through the kitchen window that had been cracked open earlier that afternoon. His stomach growled, but he knew Sandy would not let him hear the end of it if he left the job unfinished. With a final burst of energy, he rushed to finish the monotonous role of cutting and hauling the last of the logs.

But a moment later, he suddenly stopped what he was doing and watched as a green Honda Civic drove past his driveway. The car moved slowly, as if the occupants were lost or looking for something. It was rare anyone drove down Piper Street, save for the few residents that lived on either side of him. It was a dead end.

Everyone knew to avoid what lied beyond the 'No Trespassing' sign that hung from a rusted chain between two posts, blocking the entrance to a crumbling, overgrown road. Occasionally, curious high schoolers stopped by to take a look, using binoculars to see what they would not dare visit on foot, but no one ever crossed the chain. At least, almost no one. The only adventurers known to ever disregard the order came from Philly or Pittsburgh, either oblivious or apathetic to the rumors that the locals shared at the pub on Friday nights or the gossip that occupied the chatter of mom's groups.

A young man exited the vehicle and removed one side of the chain, setting it and the 'No Trespassing' sign gently to the ground, as if attempting to compensate for a wrong he was about to commit. The Civic continued on and out of sight, save for the occasional flashes of headlights beyond the trees. Josh set down his ax and ran inside to tell his wife of the news; the old, abandoned hospital had visitors.

Sandy set the plates on the counter and peered out the kitchen window. She wanted to know every detail, from who was driving to where the plates were registered. Nothing ever happened in Pennsdale, and the presence of someone new…*there*…was enough to become the talk of the town. Sandy would look out the front window with her binoculars a couple of times in the hopes of getting juicy details to share with her local women's group later that week but, to her utter dismay, could see nothing behind the tree line.

The abandoned hospital, or rather the remnants of it, sat waiting, its stately aura not lessened by the passage of time or the destruction that had occurred within its walls years before. Once bustling with activity, it found itself in an odd predicament of loneliness, a type of purgatory it seemed cursed to endure. It had not seen a visitor in years, except for stray cats and vermin. It was kept hidden from society, as the locals desired it to be, found only by the lost or thrill seekers.

The building nearly shook with shock at the break in silence it had become so accustomed to. Could it be? No, surely not. But yes, it was…the sound of an engine off in the distance came again. Bright headlights appeared behind the rows of trees, disappearing and then reappearing. One might assume, and rightly so, that they would turn around, yet the vehicle grew closer until its headlights turned to face the front of the two-story, red brick structure, casting an eerie glow within the rooms and shadows against the walls, as if life once again roamed around within. The foreign sound of the engine approaching spooked even the crows, who flew up in a dark swarm towards the safety of the sky, unsure whether the approach signaled a threat.

The Civic came to a stop about fifty feet before the front steps, unable to traverse the remainder of the road which, warped by roots and harsh weather, had become impassable. Three teenagers exited, stretching their arms and legs and grabbing full backpacks from the trunk. A girl with brown hair that fell to her mid back vigorously rubbed her arms, her blue knit sweater not nearly warm enough for the chilly evening. Two slightly older boys in hoodies stood beside her, silently studying the hospital, as if evaluating whether whatever history they knew about it matched their initial impression.

"This is it?" the girl asked, a tone of disappointment evident in her voice. Based upon the stories she had heard, she had expected something more in line with the Addams Family home, not some innocuous building that appeared no more threatening than a neglected, old schoolhouse. Jamie Parkins hoped she had not just driven an hour for nothing. Saturday evenings at sixteen were rife with parties and sleepovers, and she suddenly regretted having passed up both in order to see the supposedly-haunted asylum that, so far, failed to impress. The group had visited several haunted sites that looked much scarier than this one.

"Well, what did you expect?" scoffed one of the young men, his short blonde hair mostly hidden under his hoodie. Andy and Jamie shared the same pale blue eyes and wide smiles and, despite the ten-inch height difference, were easily recognizable as siblings.

"Don't worry. It'll be worth it once we get inside," Nick Foster assured her, running his hand through his dark hair as he studied the asylum. "But it's probably going to take some time to find anything in this place. It's huge," he said, looking around at the expansive property. He seemed confident enough that it was going to be a successful night and turned on the flashlight feature on his phone, eager to begin the ghost tour. The others quickly followed suit.

Whatever other doubts Jamie had she kept to herself. Perhaps she would be pleasantly surprised by a slamming door or audio recording of a lost soul. If it could happen at the old mill and the shuttered hotel, it could happen here, too. It was the thrill of witnessing something unexpected that surpassed any other ghost-hunting experience. The three walked towards the front door, the darkness of the evening quickly setting in.

"Nick, did you bring the Ouija board?" Jamie asked.

"Of course. And the recorder and EMF meter," he said, glancing in his backpack. "Oh yeah, and the map." He pulled out a sheet of paper with a hand-drawn blueprint of the hospital and its grounds. "Always prepared," he said boastfully.

Andy let out a laugh and glanced at Jamie to see whether she shared in his amusement.

"What?" Nick asked, not seeming to understand.

"I just think it's funny. That's all."

"What's so funny?" Nick was not happy to be the butt of an unknown joke, especially when he realized Jamie was hiding a smile.

Andy sighed. "Always prepared, huh? Like when you forgot your recorder at the Brightenton Jail Museum and your backpack at Hill View Manor?" He gave Nick's shoulder a teasing nudge.

"Better than forgetting the car keys at…what's that old cabin near Spring Mills?" he quipped. He had neglected to tell the group about losing his senior class ring at the old orphanage or getting the ghost hunting team lost on more than one occasion because he could not find his map. Andy already knew and would have teased him further but was drawn in by what lied before them.

With each step forward, the old mental hospital became more ominous and intimidating, daring them to continue. It towered above them, as if they were tiny ants invading a large castle, threatening to absorb them right up. The two-story façade stood flanked by double wings that extended out past the center of the building like wings on a dragonfly and gave the structure a hulking appearance that one could not take in entirely without rotating themselves. Rows of windows spanned the exterior, many broken or missing. A few here and there appeared to have bars on them. The roof was riddled with holes, a victim of the elements and neglect. The roofline above the entryway showcased an impressive, clover-shaped gable with a lone window. Jamie noticed a small teddy bear sitting beside the glass, and she felt herself shiver, though this time not from the cold. She thought she saw the face of a little boy, too, but just as quickly as it appeared, it vanished. Unsure whether her eyes were playing tricks on her, she chose to say nothing about it to the others. She did not need them making fun of her for being afraid, though she was quite sure from the look on Andy's face that he had seen something as well.

A triple archway, separated by concrete columns, stood at the entrance, and eight feet or so beyond were large double doors, black and heavy and covered in years of grime. A metal plaque beside the doors read 'Chastain Park Psychiatric Hospital, Est. 1874.' A second plaque below continued, 'Home for Imbeciles, Epileptics, and the Insane.' Cobwebs and abandoned birds' nests occupied the corners of the vestibule, and the floor was covered with the remnants of dead insects and bird droppings. The trio wondered quietly how bad the inside would be.

It was not often they visited abandoned buildings. They preferred the ghost hunts that cost a few dollars for entry and were predictably scary. But having visited all of the local haunts within driving range, they were eager for something new. It had been Andy's idea to visit the asylum, and he had convinced Nick after English class to join him and Jamie that weekend. He had heard rumors that the old mental hospital was haunted and, in his research, discovered that a horrendous fire had claimed the lives of at least ninety-two people in the 1950s.

Nick turned the knob anxiously, running his other hand across his wet brow, unsure whether he would have to pick the lock, and breathed a sigh of relief when the door effortlessly swung open. It ceased to amaze him how nearly every abandoned building they had visited was left carelessly unlocked, as if welcoming in vagrants and vandals. He gave a little laugh at his luck.

"Ladies and gentlemen, welcome home," he joked, gesturing the siblings into the building.

A peculiar smell of charred wood and dampness greeted them at the door. They shone their lights into the darkness, horrified to find cobwebs stretching in thick cotton sheets from the light fixtures to the crumbling leather sofas in what appeared to be a lobby of sorts. Andy exited the building, returning a short time later with sticks for each of the tourists, much to the relief of Jamie, who, in particular, hated spiders and had no desire to walk through any webs.

"So, where to first?" Andy asked. He glanced at Nick's blueprints and could see that he had already circled a hallway labeled 'Insane' in red pen. "Nice," he responded in affirmation. If there was any area of the building that was haunted, that was sure to be it.

"I thought we'd start out up there, towards the back of the hospital, and then make our way to the morgue for the séance." Nick almost seemed giddy with excitement as he described how the morgue sat almost directly below the quarters used for the insane and how the prospect of having the dead below them likely did not help their mental stability.

"Hey, look at this," Jamie called from across the room. She had wandered to the doorway in the back and was only noticeable by her phone's light, which she shone towards an unseen space ahead. They wandered over to where she stood and, only then, noticed the disgusted look on her face. A collection of antique children's toys lied before them, nearly hidden behind thick cobwebs and long since forgotten. Flattened balls littered the floor, having not bounced in decades. A lone sneaker, its laces untied, lied on its side, its white sole nearly completely masked by dark charring. And remnants of deceased vermin, mummified and stiff and looking eerily similar to the stuffed toy animals beside them, lied scattered across the floor, as if one and the same.

"Gross!" exclaimed Jamie, nearly gagging.

A stench of lingering decay remained and, mixed with the scent of burnt wood and damp furnishings, smelled like an odd combination of wet sneakers and rotten meat. A few paintings still clung to the wall, crooked, their frames splitting apart at the corners. They depicted farms and rolling hills or family portraits, as though taunting the patients who would never experience such life luxuries. The teenagers quickly walked through the long room, stepping on animal remnants and dried feces and swatting at stray webs, not caring to examine the details further. It was a sad room. It had been an adult hospital, yet clearly used to house the mentally disabled who did not mature past childhood. Jamie felt sorry for those who had lived their lives in this prison.

The group passed what had been an administration hall off to the right and a dining hall to the left. At the end of the room lied a second set of halls for epileptics and imbeciles, the women's quarters to the right and the men's to the left. The trio had finished reading *The Shame of Pennsdale* the night before, which described the separation as a way to prevent pregnancies among patients. Just beyond the halls was another double door with a plaque reading 'Therapy Pool' above.

"Do you know where we're going?" Jamie asked nervously. Burnt wood beams hung precariously from the ceiling, threatening to pull the floor above down with it at the slightest provocation. And the stench of the room was starting to make her queasy.

"Of course," Nick responded, giving her a contrived look of insult. As if leading the group on a tour, he entered the pool room, the pool now nothing more than a dry concrete hole, undeterred by the crumbling walls beside him. He continued, holding his light under his chin and illuminating his face, "This is the pool that was used for physical therapy. A mentally-handicapped patient by the name of Casper Stevens drowned here in 1950, but rumor has it that a staff member murdered him. His ghost still roams these halls, looking for someone to help him." He let out an unexpected yell in feigned fright, piercing the silence that followed his brief story, and Jamie screamed, nearly tumbling backwards into the hole.

Andy caught her arm and cast Nick an eye roll. That was just the sort of thing Nick would make up. He was lucky she had not fallen in, or it would have been a slug to the gut.

"That wasn't funny," Jamie responded, giving Nick's shoulder a light punch.

Nick struggled to hide a smile. "Sorry, Jamie."

He liked Andy's little sister. She was cute. The two had made out once at a party but had been careful to hide it from Andy. He was protective of Jamie and would not have approved of her hooking up with his best friend. But sometimes, the two would pass notes during physics or hang out on the bleachers after school. They were beginning to feel a little like Romeo and Juliet with their sneaking around. Andy seemed oblivious to the whole thing and, even now, did not notice the way Nick and Jamie looked at each other. His sole focus was on the blueprints, which he eagerly studied under the light of his phone, looking for one stairwell in particular.

"Guys," he motioned, "this way."

They filed out the doors and under the 'Therapy Pool' plaque, turning towards the women's unit and then through a heavy, fire-proof door that slammed shut behind them. Unlike the other rooms, the stairwell seemed preserved in time, unaffected by the fire that had once ravaged the building and immune to critters. If one had not known any better, they might expect to walk out the door and onto a bustling patient ward. Yet it felt ominous. The air was thick and heavy and had an electrical charge that seemed to grow with each step towards the next floor, as if waiting to zap them at any moment. It seemed as if the eyes of something unseen bored into them, watching their approach, daring them to step one foot closer. They could all feel it and wanted to turn back, but they had driven all the way out here specifically to see what sat beyond this particular stairwell. There was no turning back.

Nick reached into his backpack and pulled out the recorder.

"Is someone here?" he asked, and after a minute of silence, played it back. No response. "Who are you?" he tried again, to which only the sound of their own heavy breathing followed.

They continued up the final steps to the second floor, pulling open the heavy door. A cold burst of wind came with it, as if a large air bubble had been pent up and was waiting to escape to freedom. But from where?

"What was that?" Andy asked, caught completely off guard by the event. No one answered. The three looked uncomfortably at each other, eventually rationalizing it as a draft from one of the many holes in the roofing.

The door slammed shut behind them, and suddenly, there was only silence. The long hallway sat in total darkness. Andy shone his light around the area. The lime-green paint peeled from the walls in large sheets, piling on the floor, and dead vermin scattered the floor and counters of the nurses' station. Water puddled here and there under damaged roofing, and a few holes on the floor sat waiting like traps, ready to break the ankle of anyone who dared pass. Patient charts littered the floor, and several red binders were cast open, revealing patient names, dates of birth, diagnoses, and physician notes.

Nick picked up a binder from his feet and curiously flipped through it.

Patient Name: Marsha Atkinson
DOB: 05/17/1923
Diagnoses: Schizophrenia, borderline personality disorder
Past Medical History: Rickets, typhoid fever, psych (as above)

2/4/53 1214

29-year-old female admitted with symptoms consistent with new-onset schizophrenia. Patient initially presented to an outside hospital, complaining of voices telling her to self-harm. Patient continues to speak of a gentleman present that neither I nor my nurses have seen. We will keep under observation for the duration of the week.
- Dr. Carl Richter

Nick flipped through the pages, stopping at a note written nearly six months later.

8/2/53 0845

Patient tolerating Chlorpromazine, 600 mg/day. No visual or auditory hallucinations reported. Attending daily group therapy sessions and making progress. Will reinstitute medication regimen, now in combination with Chlorpromazine.

- Dr. Carl Richter

Skipping to the last page…

8/18/53 0635

Patient found deceased of apparent suicide at 0601. Notified by nurse that patient found hanging from a noose consisting of bedsheets in apparent suicide. Attempted to revive but unsuccessful. Pronounced dead at 0614. Coroner and family notified. Patient to be transported to morgue.

- Dr. Carl Richter

"Whoa, guys, this is messed up. Look at this," Nick beckoned.

The siblings took turns reading through the grim tenure of Marsha Atkinson. Though the pages were yellowed with smoke and age, and the writing was the stereotypical messy cursive of a physician, they could gather that the woman had gone through many ups and downs prior to her suicide and that her medication regimen was started, stopped, and changed often.

"Does it say what room she stayed in?" Andy asked. The rooms were labeled one through ten, five rooms on the right and five on the left, on a hall that started just beyond the nurses' station.

"Room six," offered Jamie.

"Well, let's go to room six then."

Nick put the binder back where he had found it, on the floor next to a fallen ashtray and other scattered binders.

Room six sat at the end of the hall and to the left. The walls were badly damaged by fire, and a partially broken window had allowed water to seep in and rot away the wood around it. The floor was littered with remnants of dark clothing, presumably from the fallen dresser, and skeletons of birds and mice that crunched beneath their shoes. Two metal bed frames remained, orange with rust after so many years, the sheets hanging off the side, as if the former occupants had just sprung from their beds. There was an eeriness within the walls of room six, the same electric charge that was in the stairwell. Nick pulled the recorder back out of his bag, seeing a good opportunity to possibly make contact.

"Marsha, is this where you died? Are you still here?"

He hit replay. Nothing. Not even the sound of a mouse shuffling or of a single breath. All was quiet, perfectly still. For a moment, it seemed like any ordinary place…dilapidated, yes, but harmless. But then they began to feel it close enough to reach out and grab, if they so chose, that undeniable and awful presence from the stairwell. It was growing stronger and all-encompassing. They could not move. It was watching them, studying them, and reading their innermost thoughts.

"What's going on?" Jamie asked through chattering teeth.

"I don't know," Andy admitted, fear in his eyes. "Let's get out of this awful room." Nick did not hesitate to follow them towards the door, unwilling to try and show bravery on this one. He felt it, too, the nasty presence in that room, and was just as ready as the others to get out. But no sooner had they reached the door than it slammed shut with a bang that cracked the wall above the frame and sent drywall crumbling on top of their heads. Jamie screamed and frantically combed her hair with her fingers, pulling at the pieces of drywall that clung on and imparted an ashy hue. Andy dusted off his hoodie and pulled on the handle, but the door would not budge. He tried again to no avail.

"It's locked. Here, you try."

Nick was stronger and more athletic than Andy but could not open the door either. He pulled his driver's license from his wallet, slipping it in the crack of the door, hoping to pop the lock by shimmying it through. This trick had worked several times before and was a talent he had shown off on many occasions, much to the oohs and aahs of onlookers. But to the dismay of Jamie and Andy, the card had no effect, as if the door had been deadbolted.

He sat on the floor, puzzled at his poor luck. Maybe he needed a bigger shim. He searched the room for remnants of thick paper, or an identification badge left behind in the chaos of the fire, that might do just the trick.

Jamie was beginning to wish she had not come along. Getting locked in a dead woman's room that could quite possibly cave in at any moment was not part of the plan. Another thought began to frighten her more, though. All three had lied about where they were going that night. The Parkins siblings had told their parents that they were going to Nick's, and Mr. and Mrs. Foster had no reason to doubt their son was at Andy's, as he promised to be. There would be no one looking for them until at least the morning, and even then, it would take time to figure out where they actually were. Making matters worse, they had not had cellphone reception since turning off Piper Street, as if the hospital was in a complete dead zone, and had no way to call for help.

Jamie heard it first. It sounded like a swing on a rusty playset, swishing back and forth, back and forth, in even, steady movements. Then the boys heard it, too. They turned, shining their lights behind them but saw nothing. Was the floor finally caving under their weight? Then, something beside them moved. Jamie shone her light around, her arm shaking, trying to see what it was. Nothing, still nothing…then something, as if growing in clarity before her eyes.

In front of them was a dark mass, swaying left, then right, then left with each creak and groan.

"Oh, jeez, what the hell," Andy shrieked.

Nick said nothing but stared ahead in petrified stillness, his gaze focused on the peculiar movement before them. The siblings reluctantly shone their lights at it, not wanting to see it but needing to know that it was not a figment of their imagination. Andy noticed a hand that swung with the fabric, its muscles loose and relaxed. It hung limply, as if made of rubber. Jamie saw the face, the eyes wide open but devoid of life. A noose was wrapped around the neck, and the head listed to the side.

Back and forth, back and forth. The creaks continued, getting louder, making sure no one, not even the deaf, could ignore them.

Jamie let out a blood-curdling scream. The boys seemed unable to break their stare, as if stuck in a hypnotic state, struggling to comprehend the sight before them. Andy wanted to look away but could not. Nick seemed to be in a trance, lulled by inaudible messages that grasped the full attention of the mind. It was talking to him telepathically, sharing a silent conversation meant for just the two of them. He nodded in acknowledgment. He knew what was needed. Marsha knew, too. She knew everything.

"What are you doing?" Andy yelled nervously. Nick carried a chair from the corner of the room to where the woman hung before stepping up beside her. The woman faded, leaving only the twisted bedsheet loop behind, and to their horror, he slipped it over his head.

"Nick, stop! Come on. Get down!" Jamie panicked. With a swift kick, the chair went tumbling across the room, quickly followed by the sickening crack of his neck.

"Nick!" Andy lifted his body up while Jamie quickly slipped the noose off, but there was nothing to be done. He was already gone. The siblings tried to regain a pulse, and when all energy had been expended, they moved the body to one of the patient beds until they could figure out their next step.

The door was still locked, refusing to budge in the slightest. Andy could not bear to look at Nick and turned away, holding his head in his hands. It must be a nightmare, one that he would surely wake up from any time now, the kind that would leave him drenched in a cold sweat and gasping for air. He imagined that he might even wake his parents up, telling them something along the lines that he had a bad headache, just for the comfort of their presence. He and Nick would laugh about it later, maybe even years down the road.

For a moment, Andy was convinced that it was indeed a nightmare. His heartbeat calmed, and his breathing slowed. But then, a woman's shrill laughter meant only for his ears filled the room, echoing like a ping pong ball off the walls, sending him back into a state of panic. The noise quieted, only to start back up, louder and more revulsive, in a tortuous cycle that continued on and on.

Andy seemed to be losing himself. If she had not known any better, Jamie would have thought he was a mental patient himself. He banged his head in a slow, steady rhythm against the wall and soon after, began to talk to people, people who were not there...or that she simply could not see. Andy whispered unintelligibly to someone unseen.

"Who are you talking to?" Jamie demanded.

"It's none of your business."

The whispers resumed.

"Andy...Andy, listen to me. Stop it. Please."

"We're trying to have a conversation. Shut up."

"Who are you talking about?" It was pitch black now, except for the light of Jamie's phone.

"Just leave me alone."

The hushed voices spoke more quickly now, wasting no time between Jamie's interruptions.

"Andy!" Jamie pleaded. But he paid her no attention. It was just him and Marsha now. She told him things, and he listened.

"You want me to...?" she finally heard him say, though she could not make out the end.

"Don't listen to her!" Jamie demanded.

"I don't want...okay...I will."

And before she even knew what was happening, the sound of footsteps dashed across the room, followed by the clatter of breaking glass.

"Andy!" Jamie yelled, horrified, chasing after him but too late. It was only a two-story fall, but he did not move or make even the slightest sound. A pool of red quickly encircled his head. "Andy!" she yelled again in disbelief. Jamie let out another terrified scream, loud enough that the Mabrys of Piper Street would later tell authorities the date and time they had heard it.

Then, just as suddenly as the door to the room had locked them in, it creaked open slowly, tauntingly, as if whatever evil possessed the room had accomplished its goal and had no further need for her.

She was a butterfly in a child's cage, let free when the fun had been fully extracted and it was nearly dead…and probably would die still. She bolted towards the stairs, the doors now opening with ease, her body swiveling this way and that as she struggled to find her way through the dark hospital, only to discover that her release had been a trick. The large double doors to the entryway were stuck…or locked…just like the door of room six. The doors of the administrative and dining halls were locked, too, as were those in the halls for imbeciles and epileptics. Unlike the window of room six, those downstairs were tightly locked and seemed impervious to kicking and the swings of chairs, refusing to so much as crack, and Jamie came to the unfortunate realization that her only possible way out was the basement.

The light of her phone tremored as she descended the dank, humid stairwell, revealing a floor even more damaged than those above. A large, old-fashioned kitchen stood in darkness, the cabinets and tile covered in a layer of fossilized soot. Droppings and carcasses of mice and rats lied scattered about, likely having enjoyed a feast on the food after the fire, only to find themselves fat and unable to get out through their usual holes once supplies ran dry. Jamie had no better luck in the laundry room, a simple room of charred metal washers and dryers and a bare table that probably had been used for folding. She felt herself begin to panic as she realized that there may not be a way out at all. There was only one room left and no other option than to walk through those swinging double doors and under the plaque reading 'Morgue.'

How many bodies had been pushed through those doors over the years, she wondered, and she quickly had to snub out those thoughts to continue. It was a small room consisting of refrigerated cabinets on one side and steel countertops on the other, still holding a variety of scalpels and other mysterious tools amongst the rubble.

A steel gurney lied empty in the middle of the room. Above it hung what was once a scale, similar to those in grocery stores, and Jamie nearly gagged at the thought of organs sitting within its basin. Still, no stairs or exits that she could see. The panic was growing. *There must be some way out.*

Just as she was about to give up on the basement and attempt a mitigated fall from a second-story window, she caught sight of two small egress windows, her light reflecting off of the glass like a beacon of hope. She pulled over the lone gurney and climbed atop, stretching, reaching, *begging* for the latch on the window to open. *Please, I'll do anything*, she promised, if only she could get out. The latch opened! It actually opened, and Jamie breathed a sigh of relief. A rush of wind blew in, replacing the stagnant, decades-old air within the morgue with the crisp, fresh air of the outdoors.

Though she had succeeded in opening a window, another problem stood before her. The gurney was far too short to climb from, and her eyes frantically searched for anything to stack on top. The phone's light moved around the room, pleading for a box or even a stack of papers…and then it stopped on something. And she wondered how she could have missed it when she walked in.

A chair sat not five feet from her. Of course, there was a chair. How else would a mortician sit and write notes? An odd combination of fear and relief manifested as a nervous laugh that broke the silence. But any reprieve from the situation at hand was short-lived. She noticed the outline first…a leg. She was sure it was a leg. It hung beside the chair and wore a shoe. She looked away, terrified. *Stop it*, she begged herself. In her fear, she had simply thought something was there when it was not…like the boy in the window and the woman…oh God, the woman. She needed to get out and get to a place where she could call for help. *Hurry up.* She shone the light towards the chair again, but it was not there. It had moved and now sat across the room, near the old refrigerators. *What the fuck.* She stepped towards it, ignoring a primal urge to run from the room and not look back, but stopped in her tracks. It was clearer now. There was indeed an occupant of that chair. He wore spectacles and a mid-century-style suit with a vest, and his retreating, gray hair sat neatly combed to one side. His white mustache was neatly trimmed. She clenched her eyes shut, and when they reopened, the man was looking directly at her. He adjusted his spectacles, as if studying his prey.

"I've been waiting for you." The voice was clear. There was no mistaking the words.

"Who…who are you?" she stuttered.

"There, there. Don't be afraid. You're home."

She shook her head. "No, you don't understand. My brother and his friend need help. I need to help them!"

"Shhh, calm down, child. You need to sleep now." He stood up and walked closer.

Jamie stepped back, nearly falling backwards onto the counter and its tools. A fear ran through her body. Who was this man? What would he do to her?

"Get away from me."

He reached out to grab her, and she screamed.

"Get away. No!" She swatted at him.

"You must rest. Just relax."

Before she could fight back, the man stuck her with something. She saw the syringe in his right hand as he lowered it and set it on the counter.

"Just calm down now." She felt herself going limp. He lifted her onto the cold gurney, and within seconds, she was out.

Samantha Robinson seemed visibly relieved when the emergency room physician entered the room. She stood beside Jamie, waiting to give her bedside report, every few seconds checking to make sure the teenager was still asleep. She had been her roughest patient all week, the fifth violent one in the last two days. Four more hours, she reminded herself, looking at the clock. Four hours until she could start her three-day weekend and be free of her duties.

"Dr. Bowman, this is a sixteen-year-old female presenting with altered mental status following a supposed ghost-hunting tour. Police were called to the shuttered Chastain Park Psychiatric Hospital after neighbors reported a trespassing vehicle and subsequent screaming. They found her in the morgue, claiming that her brother and his friend were dead. However, officers failed to locate anyone else on the premises. While speaking with her parents, officers were informed that her brother and his friend were home all evening and had no idea she was visiting the hospital alone. The patient also claims that a mortician sedated her in the morgue, although it is suspected that this "mortician" was actually a paramedic. Since arrival, she has experienced visual and auditory hallucinations and does not remember her name. She has been agitated and combative and was administered Lorazepam. She hit me," the woman showed him a red mark on her upper arm, "and some of the other nurses."

"Gosh, I'm sorry. Are you okay?"

"Yeah, but still. It's never fun to get hit." Samantha rubbed her arm. It felt as if someone had thrown a baseball, full blast, at her. But it was just a teenage girl, and a small one at that.

"The Lorazepam ought to keep her out for a few hours. Get some ice for that," Dr. Bowman added. That was going to be some awful bruise. "I'm happy to prescribe something for you if the pain is too bothersome. Does she have any relevant past medical history?"

"None, except tonsils out at six."

"Okay, psych's been consulted. I'm sure they'll want to keep her. Probably new-onset schizophrenia. Until then, she needs a sitter. I don't want her hurting herself or someone else when she wakes up. Where are her parents now?"

"On their way."

"Good. I'd like to speak with them once they arrive."

Chapter Two

1953

"Can I bury it in the ground?" A little girl tugged the bottom of Shirley Fitzpatrick's floral-print dress, begging for a moment of attention.

"Bury what, sweetie? Did Sammy give you another worm?" She glanced across the playground towards another kindergartener, a little boy known for playing pranks on his fellow classmates.

A few pitiful cries followed. "It's dead."

"What's dead?" Shirley asked patiently. She ran her hand through her short bob, sweeping loose pieces of dark hair from her face. It was a hot day, and the sweat beaded across her forehead. The small hands were pressed together, domed around something unfortunate enough to come within their grasp. She got on her knees and gently pried them open.

"The moth!" Julia cried.

"Did you catch it?"

"Yeah, but it's not moving now."

"Did you squish it?" Shirley asked with a scrunched-up nose. One of the wings hung on only by a thread.

"It was by accident. I was going to bring it home and make it my pet."

"It's okay. Sometimes, our little insect friends don't make it. It's nothing to worry about. Here." She picked up a shovel from the sand pit. "Let's take it over here. I'll help you bury it."

Julia remained in deep mourning as they walked across the playground, where children swung high and showed off their strength on the monkey bars, to a little patch of grass. Shirley dug a few inches deep, and Julia placed the moth gently into the ground, somberly filling it with dirt, and then laid a blossomed dandelion atop.

The bell rang, and Shirley walked with her arm around Julia's back to the classroom.

"You know, you're really good at this." Mrs. Lambert was a woman in her mid-fifties and ready to retire after a career teaching kindergarteners and the young college students who would enter the teaching field. Her hair was pulled up, away from her face, and tucked neatly into an updo. Her eyes studied Shirley behind large-frame glasses.

"Well, thank you, Judy. One more year, and I'll have a class of my own."

"Maybe you'll have mine." She gave the young woman a side glance. "In fact, I'd be willing to help make that happen if you had an interest."

"Well, that'd be marvelous," she said, struggling to contain her excitement. "I mean, it might just be what I was hoping for," she added, her voice forcibly calmed.

"Can you stay a few minutes after class? I'd like to ask Mr. Hartford to join us so that I can show him some of the wonderful things you've been helping with in the classroom."

"Of course. Thank you."

Later that evening, Shirley's 1942 black Cadillac sedan pulled into the driveway of her parent's home. The car had been passed down to her after her grandfather passed away two years before, and she had made every effort to maintain its new-like condition. It was the house she had grown up in, a two-story brick home half an hour north of Philadelphia. She loved being back this time of year. Her mother's roses and hostas were in full bloom, and the grass a vibrant green after the late summer rains. She could not wait to see the large garden her mother kept that grew just about any fruit or vegetable one could imagine. Janet often bartered the excess food for the fine leather a farmer down the road produced or embroidery done by the woman across the street. Sometimes, and much to Shirley's embarrassment growing up, she brought produce with her to local shops and exchanged it for lamps, quilts, and other household items. Gardening had become a game to her mother, and each year, she sought to outdo what she had done the last. In fact, last Christmas, Janet had boasted about not spending a single penny on gifts, which covered her den floor and stacked two feet high. Her goal this year was to acquire enough teddies, trucks, dolls, and books to make Christmas at the local orphanage magical.

It was not that the family was wanting for money. The Fitzpatricks had actually done quite well. Bill Fitzpatrick ran a successful furniture company out of Philadelphia. He bought Amish furniture from rural communities at a discount and then resold the pieces to city dwellers for a steep markup. Business was good. He had recently expanded to five stores across the Northeast and hoped to add two more in the South. Everyone wanted the sturdy, handmade furniture he was selling.

"Darling, you're home!" A woman in her late forties greeted Shirley on the front walkway. She wore khaki slacks and a short-sleeved blouse, smeared with dirt along the front.

"Whoa, watch the dessert." The carrot cake nearly tumbled out of Shirley's arms as the two embraced.

"How was the drive? Not bad, I hope."

"It was a nice drive. I need to try and get out here more often. It looks wonderful with all of the flowers.

"You'll have to excuse this," she pointed at her clothing. "I've been outside all afternoon. Come see the garden."

"I was just going to ask."

They dropped off the carrot cake in the kitchen. The house smelled of baked casserole and fresh coffee.

"Your father will be home in about half an hour. He found some cabinetry he just had to have but promised he'd try and hurry." Janet took a step back, looking Shirley up and down. It was a short-sleeved summer dress that ran just below the knee and highlighted the hip with a thin pink belt, which matched the floral-patterned material. "That is a fine dress! Did you make it?"

"No, I had it made over at Needles and Threads. Isn't it a delight?"

"It sure is. I might have to go over there myself."

Janet led the way out back to the garden. What once upon a time had been a green lawn and swing set was now row after row of fruits and vegetables. Towards the front were the tomatoes, carrots, beans, lettuce, cucumbers, and cauliflower. Then there were the rows of berries and herbs, and all the way in the back was a small orchard with two rows of apple trees. Every time she visited, there was something new, and this time, Shirley spotted a long row of roses up against the fence.

"Those are new," she observed.

"You wouldn't believe what a demand there is for fresh flowers. Last weekend, I supplied all of the roses for a wedding in town."

"Did the bride and groom pay you in rice?" Shirley asked jokingly.

"No, actually, I did it for free."

"For free?" Shirley had never seen her mother turn down a trade of some sort.

"Yes."

"But why?"

"It was a teenage couple with a baby on the way. I just thought it'd be a nice wedding gift," she responded modestly.

"Well, that was thoughtful of you." Shirley suddenly felt a pang of sadness. It seemed to happen every time a wedding was brought up.

The sound of a car engine came from the driveway, and the women walked back up to the house. Janet excused herself and reemerged a few minutes later, wearing clean clothes. Meanwhile, Bill and Shirley had sparked up a conversation over coffee.

"Daddy tells me that you two are going to Italy. When are you going?"

"In October. We were actually hoping you would like to go with us." A moment of silence passed, and Janet's smile faded when she realized the enthusiastic 'yes!' she had expected was not coming. "What's the matter, dear? Don't you want to go?"

"I'd love to, but I can't. I've got school and exams and a fundraiser to host for the sorority."

"It would be a nice family trip, just for a week. We're going to see the Sistine Chapel, the Colosseum, and the Vatican. I'm sure your instructors would understand," Bill said knowingly. He set his hands on his round belly, gave an encouraging, jovial smile, and then tapped his cigar on the ashtray. "Just tell them you'll make the work up when you get back."

"It's not that easy, unfortunately. I'm afraid I just can't." As the first in the family to attend college, she often found herself having to defend attending class when it interfered with friendships and family time…and dating. Bill and Janet were beginning to worry that their daughter was not married like most of her high school peers. Some of her old friends were already pregnant with their second child. Their worst fear was that she would end up alone, without anyone to provide for her or to give her a family. She was young and pretty and had drawn the attention of many fellow students at the University of Pennsylvania, but the relationships did not last once it became clear that Shirley desired to have a career outside of the home.

Her latest breakup with Sean Mackey had been a considerable blow, more to her parents than Shirley. They had met at a party and dated for a year. But as had been the case many times before, when conversations about abandoning career aspirations arose, it came to an end. She was part of a new generation of women who wanted everything…the husband, the kids, and the successful career. It was not that she looked down upon those friends, or even her own mother, who lived differently, but she was cut from a different cloth and could not imagine herself happy staying home all day, cooking, cleaning, ruffling through home decorating magazines, and playing bridge with other neighborhood women. She also did not want to be financially trapped like her grandmother had been should a marriage go south.

"Well, if that's what you want, I suppose it will just be us." Bill smiled at his wife. "But maybe you'll change your mind and keep us old folks company."

"You hardly qualify as old folks," she laughed. "I'm sure you'll have a marvelous time, just the two of you, and won't miss having me there at all. In other news," Shirley continued, eager to change the subject before they convinced her to go, "I've been offered a job!"

"What? Where?" Janet asked.

"Well, this afternoon, in fact, I was offered the position of kindergarten teacher over at Adams Elementary. I'll start next fall. Isn't that grand?"

"That's marvelous. Nicely done," Bill congratulated.

"How wonderful! We are proud of you," Janet added. It was the truth, despite their reservations about her career aspirations. Their hard-working daughter had achieved her life-long goal of becoming a teacher. Though even as she uttered those words, she felt a tinge of sadness.

"Now, where's that casserole I've been smelling?" Bill rubbed his stomach impatiently. "I'm starved."

Sean Mackey and Shirley Fitzpatrick had been two peas in a pod. He had really loved her, so much so that his entire world revolved around his studies and her. Janet loved him, too. He was exactly what she had envisioned for her daughter…a studious young man who planned to attend medical school and came from a good family. He wore his brown hair slicked into a deep side part, his face cleanly shaven, and was never seen without a button-down shirt and tie. Sean looked the picture of class and success. He would surely have provided a stable home for her daughter to raise a family. It did not hurt that both he and Bill were Kentucky Derby fans and enjoyed duck hunting.

Sean and Shirley had met at a Kappa Sigma fraternity party. Shirley was a member of the Alpha Chi Omega sorority, and it was common for the two chapters to intermingle. He could not take his eyes off the beautiful Shirley Fitzpatrick, who looked strikingly similar to Elizabeth Taylor, and would have done just about anything for her.

One evening in early June, the two had packed up sandwiches, fruit, and wine and set out for a picnic by the local river. The crickets chirped loudly, and lightning bugs illuminated the growing shade of evening. The water was higher than usual after a recent rain storm, and the shoreline far narrower, licking the edges of the quilt from time to time. The water seemed to sing a hushed lullaby as it flowed through the wildlife, adding a peaceful element to the chaotic cacophony of sounds.

"So, you know I start medical school in August?" Sean asked, stating the obvious fact that loomed over Shirley's mind now more than ever. He would be leaving Pennsylvania for Washington state in less than two months. Being unmarried, it was assumed she would remain behind and lie in wait, patiently, as he completed his next degree.

"Of course. And I will fly out whenever I can," she promised. Though optimistic about their relationship, her happiness for him came with a dose of dread and sadness and always the nagging fear of what would happen when the time came for him to leave.

He squirmed a bit. His palms were clammy, and cheeks flushed, the way they always did when he was nervous. Shirley noticed, and her heart sank as her mind struggled to suppress the suspicion of an impending breakup. And just as suddenly as all seemed lost…

"What do you think about coming with me?"

"To Washington? That'd be marvelous, though Mother and Daddy would never approve."

"I mean, as my wife. Shirley Fitzpatrick, will you marry me?" Sean looked at her hopefully, his eyes begging for an answer in the affirmative. For a moment, all went silent. The crickets ceased chirping, the cicadas went quiet, and even the water tiptoed around them, as if nature itself was waiting for the response.

"What about school? I still have a year."

"You wouldn't have to worry about that anymore. Don't you see? You could stay home. We could start a family. You don't really want to be a career woman, do you?"

When she had started college, she had not. Finding someone to marry was what was expected of her…and what she wanted. Women only worked when they absolutely needed to. But as time passed, she found herself desiring a career she could be proud of and wanted to spend it helping children. She could manage it all, she had told herself…the career, the house, the husband, the kids. Plenty of women juggled it all these days…well, some at least…and why should she be any different than them?

"I do."

"You want to be a career woman, or you want to marry me?" Sean asked, genuinely confused.

"I want both."

"You can't do both. How would you work all day and still clean, cook, do laundry…raise kids?"

"I will make it work. Plenty of women do."

Sean did not seem convinced. No women in his family worked. It would be an embarrassment. A woman's place was in the home, for goodness' sake.

They sat for a moment in awkward silence, neither knowing how to proceed. The wildlife could hold its breath no longer, and a flood of chirps and whistles and hisses rushed in. A lone turtle sat on a branch, facing them, still watching the drama that unfolded before him and unwilling to relinquish his front-row seat.

He pulled the box out of his pocket.

"Shirley, I don't know what to say, except that I love you and want to marry you." He had a boyish look about him, as if pleading with someone to play ball and confused about why they would not. And then, a feeling of intense guilt overcame Shirley. How could she be so cruel? How many times does one have a wonderful man propose to them? Certainly, they could figure out the details later, when there had been time to think.

"I'm sorry. Of course, I will marry you!" she replied bashfully.

It was the response he had hoped for, and his look of confusion quickly gave way to a look of relief.

"I thought for a moment you were going to turn me down and make me return my ring," he said with a laugh, slipping a simple, round-cut diamond onto her finger. The last glimmers of light hit the facets, creating a disco ball of colors.

"Why, it's beautiful." She held her hand towards the dimming sun, studying the sparkling rainbows.

"Not half as beautiful as you." He leaned over and kissed her hard, untying the bow at her waist.

"Stop it," she laughed. "Here?" She doubted anyone would come across them, but still, what if? It was getting dark. There would be no one. He slipped her dress over her head, and she unbuttoned his shirt, careful to place it out of the dirt. He laid her down on the ground gently, and they blended in with the nature around them, just two more creatures amongst the mix.

For several days after their engagement, neither brought up Shirley's school or career plans, living in blissful denial of a rather serious threat to their relationship, but within weeks, their interactions had devolved into constant quarreling. Sean had hoped he could convince her to leave school behind, but Shirley just would not budge. He grew more and more irritated with her stubbornness. It had finally come to a head over dinner one night. The two sat quietly at his apartment kitchen table, eating the spaghetti that Shirley had brought over. She looked down at the ring as it swung loosely around her finger, righting it before the diamond slipped back behind her finger again. The band was too big, and she had not had the time to have it resized yet. She did not try to fix it this time and left the diamond on the backside of her hand.

They had spent the afternoon squabbling over future plans. Both families were ecstatic about the engagement and had pressured the two to set plans for an end-of-summer wedding, just in time for the move. But the rush also meant an urgency to settle the problem of Shirley's sudden career drive. And by the time they sat down for dinner that night, neither was willing to concede. What before had seemed such a minor discrepancy had now become a point of fierce contention, each easy to anger over the other's perception of married life. Both so eagerly wanted to settle the problem and were growing increasingly frustrated at the realization that they could not come to a happy agreement.

The ring slipped off, making a noticeable clank on the wooden table and breaking the silence. Shirley hurriedly placed it back on her finger. Sean didn't look up from his plate. In fact, nothing was said until a simple 'goodbye' some fifteen minutes later.

The following day was not better. The difference was driving a stark wedge between them. Every subject inevitably returned to Shirley's career and whether or not it was suitable for a woman to pursue a career while married. It was like driving around in circles, trying to find a way out but only returning to the same spot over and over again. It was enough to make even the sanest feel as though they had lost their minds. They began spending more time apart until it got to the point that neither had any interest in seeing the other. Their relationship had become toxic. Eventually, the ring found its way back to the ring box and then, soon after, to the ring shop, where it was returned for a sharp reduction in value.

Jasper's was the local fish and chips restaurant on campus where students who wanted to avoid the questionable dining hall food hung out. A crowd of youngsters filled the outdoor picnic tables, chatting away in a pleasant hum over food and soda. Doris Day's *It's Magic* played softly over the speakers.

Abby Fletcher told anyone who bothered listening about her recent trip to France and bragged about how good the food there had been. Shayna Marshall, a shy, young woman, smiled and nodded, feigning interest in a conversation she cared little about. But Abby was the only friend of the bunch who had shown up that evening, so she was stuck. A group of college boys sat one table over, discussing the engine of the new Buick Skylark. And next to them, a group of girls and their dates busily finished their meals, rushing to catch a drive-in movie. Shayna glanced over at the group, wishing she was with them instead.

Bonnie Stevens waited for them to get up before snatching the table for herself. Two sodas and cardboard boxes of food sat before her. She looked at her wrist…six forty-five. Shirley had said six thirty. Maybe something had come up. A few more minutes passed. Then, the boys sitting at the table beside her turned their heads and watched as Shirley walked past them, giving Abby and Shayna a courteous wave as she sat down. She was stunning, and neither stopped gawking until Bonnie shot them a glare back.

"Hi there. Look at that dress!" Bonnie commented. It was the same floral dress she had worn to her parents' the week prior. Never in her life had an item of apparel held so much popularity.

"Why, thank you. I keep having people ask me about it. I'm starting to think I need to offer it to the highest bidder," she joked. The two embraced.

Bonnie was a few inches shorter and blonde. She was president of the Alpha Chi Omega chapter, and Shirley, the vice president of philanthropy. Although the sorority fundraiser was still months away, the two had an abundance of planning to do. The fundraiser would raise money for the Help Them Thrive foundation, established a few years prior as a means of financially supporting families in need. This year's goal was a sizeable two thousand dollars.

"So, what do you propose we sell?" Bonnie asked.

"October is not too far off from the holidays. Perhaps nice items that can be given away as gifts? Jessica loves to knit. Perhaps she could make a few blankets. Sara is a talented artist…I'm sure she would not mind working on a few paintings. Annalise makes jewelry that rivals the best jewelers. Maybe she'd be willing to make earrings and necklaces. If we could get ten dollars from even half the people in attendance, we will meet our goal."

"I like it. How very business savvy of you."

They discussed the hors d'oeuvres and drinks that would be served and decided on black tie formal attire for the evening. Invites would be posted around campus, opening up the event to students outside Greek life. After the majority of the details had been discussed and jotted down in a spiral notebook, Bonnie's cheerful voice grew somber.

"How have you been?" She placed a hand on Shirley's arm. "It's got to have been awful. I'm sorry."

"I've been well, actually." And she had been. Strangely enough, she had not given the breakup much attention. She had busied herself over the summer with different activities and, many days, found that she did not think about it at all, though there were the occasional nights at the end of summer she lied awake, wondering whether that would have been her wedding night. But any such thoughts were quickly squelched by sour memories of the relationship's end and by the relief of having, at least temporarily, escaped the predicament of societal and personal discordance. She was not going to be the homemaker her own mother had been. She wanted something different.

"I heard that Sean is dating Susie Wellington." Bonnie rolled her eyes. Susie Wellington was a stuck-up bitch and a member of the Alpha Delta Pi sorority. Her father was Senator James Wellington, a democrat from Harrisburg, and she made sure everyone knew it. Shirley had once had the misfortune of meeting her, and it took a shot of tequila to wash away the bitter residual of their brief conversation. Susie Wellington and Abby Fletcher were good friends, but occasionally, their narcissistic personalities clashed, forcing them into an on-again, off-again relationship. But, nonetheless, she was the homemaker type, and the more Shirley reflected on the matter, exactly what Sean was looking for.

"Cheryl told me last week," Shirley responded, her face devoid of emotion. Cheryl Watkins had been her roommate for the past two years and had witnessed, first hand, the ups and downs of the relationship.

"That was quick, wasn't it?"

"Yeah, I guess so. He's free to date whomever, though."

Shirley stopped chewing. Bonnie noticed and decided it best to drop the matter. She had merely meant to make sure she was holding up well and had not meant to upset her.

"I'm sorry. I shouldn't have said anything about it."

Shirley let out a long sigh. "It's okay, really. We left things off cordially, and I'm happy for him."

"You don't look happy, if you don't mind my saying so."

Perhaps her friend was right. For the first time in her life, Shirley felt disposable, like a glass vase that could be easily replaced should it break or go out of style. Susie was the type he wanted…a woman eager to give up everything for life in the home. She could not be mad that a match was made but, at the same time, could not shake the growing feeling that there was something wrong with her. Why was she so stubborn about finishing school? Why did she feel that she had to have a career? Why couldn't she just spend her life in the home like every other rational female she knew? Maybe she did belong in the home, and taking the teaching job was a mistake. Had she ruined her only chance of having a marriage and a family by choosing the latter?

"I'll be okay." She forced a smile.

The boys sitting at the table beside theirs had scooted their way over to Abby and Shayna, and shortly thereafter, the four got up and left together, headed in the direction of an ice cream parlor. It was already eight o'clock, and the lights outside of Jasper's flickered off, signaling to anyone left that it was time to leave. Except for Greek life activities and a small handful of businesses that stayed open past nine, the campus had an early bedtime, everyone retreating to the libraries and study halls in preparation for classes the next day.

The women took the cue and got up to leave, quickly clearing the table of leftover food and drinks.

"You look like you could use a drink. Why don't you stop by my room in an hour? I'm having a couple of friends over that I'd like for you to meet. It'd be good to get your mind off of things for a while."

"I will. Thanks."

Bonnie had to stop by a sister sorority on the way, so Shirley made the walk back alone. Had she just made the most awful mistake of her life? It was a terrifying thought that left her heavy with uncertainty.

A cool evening breeze caught the end of her skirt, sending it up high above her knees before her hands could react and push it back down. A group of young men walking past her whistled, as she buried her face, mortified. Her walking pace quickened, and when she finally reached her room at the sorority house, she slammed the door shut behind her. She was glad Cheryl was gone for the weekend. She would walk over to Bonnie's room because she had agreed to, but other than that, did not care to see anyone.

Chapter Three

Two months later, the red and gold ballroom of the Hilton Hotel was a sight to behold. Dark oak tables with red upholstered seats were beginning to fill with guests, dressed in fine suits and cocktail gowns. Glimmering crystal chandeliers floated grandly overhead, offsetting the dark ambience. Fresh flowers and tea lights adorning each table and had been set out by Shirley earlier that day. Dick Haymes' *How Deep is the Ocean?* flowed from the speakers, and the ballroom felt as though it was ready for the first dance at a wedding reception.

The space had been generously lent out to the sorority free of charge. It helped to know the manager of the hotel, a former Alpha Chi Omega member herself. For a good cause, Johanna Gibbons would do just about anything. She and Shirley had met briefly when she visited the sorority a while back to give a talk on her personal career success, as part of a broader initiative on campus to encourage women to seek employment after graduation, and Shirley had been intrigued by how she had advanced in the hotel business. Shirley had remembered where she worked and tracked her down one afternoon, just before she left work for the day, to ask if the sorority might use the ballroom for the Help Them Thrive fundraiser. Having grown up in poverty herself, Johanna was a more-than-willing supporter.

Two tables occupied the front of the ballroom, separated by a podium and bouquet of colorful balloons, displaying items awaiting auction. The first housed an assortment of knitted blankets, oil paintings, and jewelry; the second, gently-used, donated cookware, porcelain and crystal vases, and books.

Shirley had borrowed an evening gown for the event, a simple, mid-calf black dress with sleeves that sat just off the shoulder. She wore white gloves, a Christmas present from her mother years ago, and her hair had been pulled back into a tidy updo. Bonnie wore a dark-green velvet dress with a matching belt that tied into a cute bow in the back. Cheryl had chosen a blue scoop-neck gown to compliment her mother's finest pearls but at the last minute, found herself returning to the sorority house with a migraine headache.

Susie Wellington was noticeably absent, and Shirley was thankful to not run into her. It was widely rumored that she and Sean had eloped the week before and were still on their honeymoon, though no one knew for sure.

More groups of young men and women filed in until the large ballroom began to feel quite crowded. Bonnie approached the podium and addressed the crowd.

"Good evening. My name is Bonnie Stevens, and I am president of the Alpha Chi Omega sorority. I would like to thank you all for coming out on this chilly evening to help us with a very important initiative. Tonight, we raise money for the Help Them Thrive foundation, which seeks to financially support families struggling to pay for basic necessities, such as groceries, housing, water, and electricity. With your help, we are hoping to raise a staggering two thousand dollars to be split amongst three local families in need. I would like to thank Shirley Fitzpatrick, our vice president of philanthropy, for organizing the fundraiser and making it a reality. I would also like to thank the sisters of the Alpha Chi Omega sorority, who worked tirelessly to handmake and collect donated items for our auction. And a special thanks to Johanna Gibbons, who generously allowed our fundraiser to utilize this magnificent ballroom. Ladies and gentlemen, Shirley Fitzpatrick," she finished, gesturing her up to the podium.

"Well, hello. I appreciate you all coming out to support our cause. I would like to start by telling you about a little boy I met through Help Them Thrive. His name is Jake, and he's seven years old. Last year, his mother learned that she had breast cancer. She became unable to shop for groceries or take care of her home and children because of her illness, so Jake's father had to reduce his hours at work. They had very little in savings to begin with and soon found themselves struggling to pay their mortgage and buying food at their local grocer on credit. Last year, we were able to raise six hundred and fifteen dollars for Jake's family, which was enough to pay off their bills and purchase half a year's worth of groceries. Jake told me that he no longer has to worry about losing electricity or having enough food to eat. The financial burden was taken off of this family when they needed it most and made all the difference for them during a time of extreme hardship. With your generosity, we can do this again for three other families in need.

On the tables to my left and right are fine items that will be auctioned off to the highest bidder. These would make the perfect gifts for your loved ones this Christmas. We hope you'll find something that helps not just your family, but also a family like Jake's. On behalf of the Alpha Chi Omega sorority, I'd like to thank you for your support. If you all are ready, we will get started."

An energetic round of applause made its way through the room.

"First, we have this fine, impressionistic oil painting of waterlilies, reminiscent of Claude Monet's *Water Lily Pond*, painted by our very own Sara Cartwright. Starting bid is five dollars. Do I hear five dollars?"

Several attendees raised their hands.

"Do I hear six dollars?"

Three women raised their hands.

"Seven?"

The same women raised their hands.

"Eight? Nine?"

And so, it continued until Shirley asked, "Fifteen?"

Only one woman raised her hand.

"Sold to the woman in the red dress!" she exclaimed excitedly.

The woman jumped up from her seat and rushed to the front, nearly skipping with excitement, eager to claim her prize. The other two women sat with their heads lowered in humbled silence. Shirley could hardly believe it. Fifteen dollars for a single painting that likely took Sara only two hours to make.

Next up on the auctioning block was a pair of dangling earrings, created from dark red stones that shimmered like rubies under the dim lighting. One of the sorority sisters carried the earrings from table to table to give everyone a good look.

"For the second bid, we have these lovely genuine garnet earrings designed and produced by Annelise Marks. The posts are made of solid fourteen-karat yellow gold and are worth far more than the five-dollar opening bid. Do I hear five dollars?"

The hands of several gentlemen flew into the air, all eager to impress their girlfriends on Christmas morning.

"Six? Seven?... Seventeen!"

How proud her father would be when he heard how much each item was going for. It seemed that she had inherited his salesmanship after all. She could not wait to tell him once they returned from Italy.

"Garnet earrings, sold to the gentleman in the blue suit. Thank you very much."

A young man approached the table with a proud grin, and Shirley could tell, he had someone special in mind to give them to.

"Next, we have this fabulous rosette blanket." Shirley unfolded a crocheted masterpiece and held it up before the guests. The pink roses were set against a white and gray background and reminded her of a blanket she had once seen in a boutique window back home. "Look at that detail. A perfect gift for your mother or sister or just yourself. Do I hear five dollars? Six?... Twelve dollars, sold to the woman in the corner."

An excited young woman collected her blanket and ran back to her seat, showing it off along the way to anyone interested. Shirley wished she had been able to choose it for her mother and could picture her, wrapped up on cold nights, nursing a sherry while watching a movie. She would have loved the gardenesque theme.

"I would like to thank the Smithfield Library for their generous donation of books for our cause. We have a set of four Sherlock Holmes books for mystery lovers, starting at five dollars. Do I hear five?"

A gentleman won the bid and carried them away under his arm in the same way he likely carried his school books around. He wore a plum vest and glasses and looked to be the book worm type.

"Another blanket, this time..." Her voice trailed off. Bonnie whispered something in her ear, and Shirley quickly exited the ballroom. A few seconds of awkward silence passed before Bonnie picked up the microphone.

"I apologize for the interruption." She glanced down at some note cards. "And this beautiful gray and white striped blanket was knitted from a washable wool by our very own Dawn Miller. Do I hear seven dollars? Eight?... Fifteen? Sold to the man in the back wearing the striped suit."

Neal Simmons enjoyed working as a firefighter for Engine Eighty-one. But nights like tonight made him never want to don bunker gear again. He had joined as a volunteer firefighter in his early twenties, responding to house fires and vehicle crashes. Within two years of starting, he had become a full-time, salaried employee and had left his job as a car mechanic behind for good. By then, he and his wife, Bobbie, had two boys with another on the way, and he needed the solid pay. Now that the boys were grown and busy with their own lives, it was just the two of them living as empty nesters in a home that suddenly felt way too big for them.

At exactly six thirty-eight that evening, Bobbie had answered the phone. A man on the other line had frantically requested to speak with Neil. Bobbie quickly ran to grab him from the garage where he had been fixing up his 1938 Dodge pickup truck that he rarely drove but repaired on his time off, hoping to restore it to pristine condition. He grabbed only a Fedora as he ran out the door to the fire station, which happened to be just three houses down, yelling to Bobbie that there had been a major accident and that he would be back when he could.

Sirens soon filled the autumn air, sending residents to their windows. It was rare anything exciting happened in the typically-quiet coastal community of Lakewood, New Jersey. Bobbie watched as the first firetruck drove down Anchor Street, quickly followed by a second and then a third. After the last firetruck had been dispatched, she wept with the realization that something truly horrific had just happened in her neighborhood.

Little Marshall Lee Thomas lived down the street and watched the red lights blaze by his bedroom window. He picked up a toy firetruck, and drove it along the glass, saying wee woo in synchrony with the passing sirens. He wondered where they were going. He stood on his bed, which sat a few feet back, for a better look and squealed with delight when he saw it. It was a big fire. It was off in the distance, but there was no mistaking the bright red flames and dark clouds of smoke that billowed up toward the sky. Oh boy, he thought. Just wait until I tell Marcy and Jack about this. Just then, an explosion sent flames even higher, and he could hear a fresh set of fire engines drive by a couple streets over.

Mrs. Beningsworth had just loaded groceries into the trunk of her new Cadillac Eldorado when she heard the sirens go by. She had to get home and fix supper for her family and did not pay much attention until the hum of the sirens had gone on for several minutes. What in the world, she wondered. As she drove the two miles back home, she could see dark smoke clouds coming from the direction of her home. She stepped on the gas, her heart pounding, suddenly fearing that one of the children had finally managed to turn on the gas stove and, God forbid, lit a match. Her foot stomped down on the accelerator harder. She did not care whether she got a ticket. Something was wrong. The smoke clouds grew thicker, almost blocking her vision of the road entirely as she approached, and she could smell it…the unmistakable stench of burning fuel. Oh God, she thought. What have they done? Her car came to a screeching halt in front of a firetruck sitting just beyond her driveway.

"Ma'am, I'm going to have to ask you to turn around."

"That's my house, right behind you." She frantically pointed at the two-story farmhouse. "Oh, thank God." She ran up to four children, aged five to fifteen, standing by the mailbox. "What is going on? Sammy? Albert? What have you done?"

"We haven't done anything," two teenage boys seemed to say in unison.

"Where's your father?"

"He's still at work. We didn't do anything. I swear," the youngest defended. She wore a purple dress with yellow flowers, mostly covered by an oversized sweater.

"Ma'am," the firefighter started.

"Carol."

"Carol," he corrected. "I'm afraid you can't go in your house right now. There's a downed aircraft on your property."

"A what?" She could not believe what she was hearing.

"A plane crashed about ten minutes ago into the fields behind your house. It's too dangerous to be here. Is there someplace else you can go?"

"My goodness! A plane crash, you said?" She was hearing, but not fully comprehending, what he was telling her.

The firefighter was quiet, but his eyes told her what she did not want to hear.

"Children, hop in the car," Carol commanded. "We're going to your aunt Claire's."

"Neal, I need you over here now," a voice from afar called, and the firefighter quickly left towards the fiery flames.

Bobbie flipped the news on…and then off…and then on…and then off again, wanting to know, but not wanting to either. It was bad, and she could not bear to watch for more than a minute at a time, knowing that her husband was in the middle of it all.

A news correspondent talked, fire and balls of smoke behind him. "A passenger jet carrying one hundred sixty-two passengers and five crew members enroute from Philadelphia to Rome, Italy has crashed in eastern New Jersey shortly after takeoff. First responders have been on the scene for approximately forty minutes. American Airlines flight 237 took off from Philadelphia International Airport at six twenty-one this evening, crashing about fifteen minutes later into the countryside of the small town of Lakewood, which sits only minutes from Point Pleasant."

Bobbie quickly switched off the television. She busied herself for a few minutes in the bathroom, rolling her graying hair with curlers. She washed her face and brushed her teeth, then brushed them again. There was nothing she could do except wait. A few minutes later, she flipped the television back on.

"We are live from the site where an American Airlines flight has crashed into the town of Lakewood, New Jersey. Residents I've spoken with have expressed shock that something so horrific occurred in their small town where, I'm told, nothing bad ever happens. This evening, we had the opportunity to speak with the local fire chief about what crews are uncovering at the crash site."

The camera switched to Mark Shilling, a neighbor in his mid-fifties whom she and her husband knew well. He and Neal spent much of their free time at the station discussing football and their children, who were roughly the same ages and had attended school together.

"Well, John, we have, unfortunately, discovered some fatalities but are holding out hope that there are survivors. Our work has been slowed by the extensive fire in the fuselage."

She shut off the television again. She turned it on only once more that evening and watched just enough to learn that there were significant casualties and that President Eisenhower would request all government entities lower the flag to half-staff the following day.

Hours later, the silence was broken by the sound of the garage door opening. It was nearly four in the morning, and Bobbie had been up all night, waiting and worrying. She scrambled to unwrap the turkey and cheese sandwich she had stored away in the fridge, then set the sandwich on one of her porcelain plates before reaching into the cellarette for the scotch. The kitchen door opened, and a gentleman with graying hair, face covered in dried sweat, blood, and soot, stood, looking as though the life had been sucked right out of him. She quickly poured the scotch and handed it to him, not knowing quite what to say. Never in their marriage had a call come in as traumatic as the one that evening. He downed the entire glass and set it on the counter. He had not eaten since lunch, and hours in a heavy suit, lifting debris and victims from the wreckage, had drained every last ounce of energy. His body slumped into the chair, his shoulders hunched over the table, barely able to hold his head up.

"Do we have any soda?" Neil asked, gesturing towards the fridge. Bobbie scuttled off, returning with a Coca Cola. He took a bite of his sandwich but could not swallow it. A sudden sense of guilt overcame him. What right did he have to eat a meal when so many others would never eat again? He set it down and stared off into a space. Then he ran to the bathroom, and Bobbie could hear him throw up. He returned a few minutes later.

"Just throw it away."

She put her hand on his shoulder. "I'm so sorry, honey."

His voice cracked as he spoke. "It was awful. Everywhere, there were pieces of plane, seats, and luggage. And the bodies…there were bodies everywhere. Men, women, children…all dead, limbs ripped off, burnt. Never have I seen so many people and heard so much silence."

Neither slept that night. The sleepless nights would become routine for Neal, who could not dismiss the utter destruction that had unfolded before his eyes. He wished he could lose the memories of what he had seen…the gray-haired, grandmotherly-type woman dressed in a long, floral dress, miraculously still wearing her bifocals; the man in his thirties, who looked unscathed and like he was sleeping, except for the lack of a left arm; the body whose torso was contorted in a supernatural form that left the hips twisted nearly three-hundred-and-sixty degrees, like a sponge being wrung out over the sink. But it was the burned teddy, lying face down in the dirt, that haunted his dreams the most.

After her abrupt exit from the podium, Shirley was led by a hotel concierge to the front desk.

"I'm sorry to bother you, Ms. Fletcher, but the caller insists it's urgent. They refused to tell me anything more."

"Hello, this is Shirley Fletcher. With whom am I speaking?"

"Ms. Fletcher, this is Charles Baker, a representative from American Airlines. There has been an emergency aboard one of our aircrafts, and we are in the process of reaching out to family members, in order to keep them updated. Do you have family aboard American Airlines flight 237, flying from Philadelphia International Airport to Ciampino Airport in Rome, Italy this evening?"

"Why yes, I dropped my parents off just a few hours ago. Oh, goodness. Are they okay?"

He continued, taking no note of her question. "Are you the daughter of…" He paused for a moment as he presumably examined the passenger registry. "…a William and Janet Fitzpatrick?"

"They are my parents, yes. You said there was an emergency. What's happened?"

"It appears that their aircraft was lost by radar shortly after takeoff. Unfortunately, that's all the information I can provide for now. For the time being, I suggest staying close to your phone, as we will contact you with any updates. What, may I ask, is the best number to reach you?"

She provided the number to her sorority and gave the airline representative a solemn "thank you." Thoughts of the worst possible scenarios flooded her mind, and she immediately dialed the number to sorority. She assumed that the airlines had tracked her down by first calling that number and, once connected to Cheryl, confirmed her suspicions as true.

"Did they tell you anything when they called?" Shirley asked.

"Nothing, other than there was an emergency of some sort, and they were trying to contact family. I'm sure it's nothing," she said nonchalantly.

"They told me the plane disappeared from radar."

"Don't let it bug you too much. When my father flew as an airman during World War Two, planes were lost from radar all the time. Maybe a plane was too far out or at too low of an altitude. These things happen."

It was reassuring to hear the calmness in her voice. Cheryl was always a friend when one was needed, though had the reputation of a being goodie-two-shoe. She was known to scold any sorority sister who dared wear a skirt above the knee. She enjoyed sewing her own dresses, all buttoned down along the front with wide collars at the neck. A bow matching each dress sat on her dresser table, waiting to complete the tedious hairdo of the day. Despite her sometimes-overbearing presence, Cheryl was well-liked among the others in the home.

Any peace derived from their conversation was short-lived. Shirley caught a cab and arrived home just before eight to find Cheryl hunched over on the bed, tearful and sniffling. Shirley did not even realize the television was on as she rushed to her side, letting her purse and jacket slip to the floor beside her.

"What's the matter? Is it your headache?" she asked, her brow furrowed in concern. Suddenly, her own worries were forgotten as she struggled to understand what was wrong with her roommate.

Cheryl pointed at the television. "Oh, Shirley. I'm so sorry," she sobbed, reaching out to hug her. She had met Shirley's parents on several occasions, and they had always been kind towards her. They did not deserve the fate they had met, and neither did her roommate.

Shirley turned her gaze towards the television, seeing but not quite understanding the catastrophe unfolding before her. There was footage of a fire and clouds of black, voluptuous clouds obscuring much of the scene. The news anchor seemed to speak some incomprehensible language. And then a word she did understand…fuselage. *What is happening?* She stared at the screen, trying to the best of her ability to decipher his message that was nothing more than gibberish. Then a red banner at the bottom of the screen appeared, very clearly reading: BREAKING: CRASH OF AMERICAN AIRLINES FLIGHT 237. Between the clouds emerged something that looked like an airplane's tail. The camera zoomed in. She could see a section of six or seven cabin windows, entirely intact amongst the mostly flattened wreckage, looking quite normal were it not for the billowing clouds seeping through the orifices. Was this the plane she had watched her parents board, not two hours prior? Oh, God. Were her parents behind those windows?

She collapsed to the ground, her legs unable to support her. How could this be? She had just dropped them off and even helped to carry their luggage up to the gate. The scent of her mother's perfume still lingered on her arms from their embrace before she had climbed those stairs into the plane. The fifteen dollars her father had given her for groceries sat in her purse, as did their house key and a pair of sentimental diamond earrings her mother had decided at the last minute to leave behind for safekeeping.

By morning, news channels would definitively confirm the worst fears of Americans across the country. There had been no survivors. Around two o'clock in the afternoon, a mortician from Helmer Funeral Parlor called to request dental records for the Fitzpatricks, but because of the poor condition of the bodies, Shirley was warned it would likely be several weeks before a positive identification was made.

Life carried on around her, though her world had stopped. She could not sleep. The thought of eating made her sick to her stomach. Attending classes and sorority functions seemed a dreadful chore. Every day became an obstacle course that she struggled to navigate. Thanksgiving came and went without much to be thankful for. The days grew shorter and darker, and her mood seemed to follow. She found herself snapping easily and falling deep into the abyss of depression, with no light at the end of the tunnel.

It was a Saturday night, and Shirley was alone in the large sorority house, which felt eerily empty and quiet. Though the other women had begged her to come along to a party down the street, she declined because of a headache, which could more accurately be described as a moodache. She had forgone dinner, but as the eleventh hour approached, her hunger could no longer be ignored. The large kitchen on the first floor had a refrigerator stocked with premade sandwiches. She grabbed a ham and cheese and then an apple from the bowl on the counter, which she proceeded to slice into fine strips. In her fatigued state, the knife slipped, cutting her arm badly enough to draw blood. Shoot. She ran to the cupboards where the first aid kit was kept and wrapped it tightly in gauze, holding pressure with her other hand. But through the pain, she felt something else. For the first time since the accident, she felt better. It was as though a wave of excitement ran through her veins, and all of her problems diminished in magnitude. When the sorority sisters returned later that evening, they were thrilled to find such an improvement in her demeanor. Perhaps Shirley was turning a corner, they mused amongst themselves.

But the gauze would become a staple in her wardrobe, and the cutting, now intentional, would continue. Whenever the others were out to a party, or late at night when everyone was in bed, Shirley would partake in her newfound self-treatment. She would sneak down to the kitchen where the knives were kept. Sometimes, the bleeding scared her. It was the times that she became lightheaded that she promised herself that she would stop. But she could not, no matter how much she wanted to.

And then, one morning, she awoke to screaming. At first, she did not know what was happening. She felt cold, really cold. She tried to sit up but fell back down. Several horrified sorority sisters gathered around, desperately trying to quell the blood loss. Minutes later, paramedics lifted her out of the blood that had pooled around her on the kitchen floor and wheeled her away, into an ambulance and to the hospital. She slipped in and out of consciousness over the following hours.

"I thought we were going to lose you," an older nurse said, wheeling over a small table with a meal of mashed potatoes, beef, and beans. "Your heart stopped twice. We've given you a transfusion. You're lucky to be alive."

Shirley picked at the food, but her bandaged arms could barely lift the fork. She set it down. Maybe she would try again later.

Nurse Beth Adams stepped out into the hallway and spoke in a whisper to the attending physician.

"Dr. Ellington, what are we going to do with her?"

"Well, she's stable. We can discharge her tomorrow to a mental health facility…that is, if one will accept her. Has family come by?"

"No. I believe her parents died in a plane crash back in October. They were on that passenger jet that crashed in New Jersey."

"Oh, how tragic. Poor girl. Is there anyone else?"

"I'll ask her again, but I don't believe so."

Dr. Ellington flipped through a stack of papers he carried on a clipboard.

"How is Mr. Salvador's leg wound healing?"

Chapter Four

Sean Mackey found out about it from Susie, who, despite having left her studies behind to follow him to medical school, stayed in close contact with several members of the Alpha Chi Omega sorority. For the next few days, it was all she talked about. She seemed to gather information by the minute, garnering juicy tidbits of information from anyone willing to contribute to her vault of gossip. It did not bother her to talk about Sean's ex-fiancé; rather, she took a particular sick joy in it all. She relished every drop of detail related to the gory events that had transpired and relayed the information with such glee that Sean found himself stepping outside every time she made a phone call. He worried about her sometimes and her obsession with the macabre.

A month prior, a woman who lived about a mile away had been murdered by her husband. News crews had swarmed the area, parking their vans along the road and gathered in groups, tripods unfolded, ready to catch any glimpse of the decedent's family. Susie refused to miss any of the action, frequently walking their dog, Bernie, two blocks over to the home of Roger and Maryanne Wilkins just for the opportunity to look at the "murder house." And every day, she relayed back the latest to Sean, who wanted to discuss anything but that darned house. But he kept his mouth shut and listened patiently, feigning enthrallment with her latest detective work. One day, she had seen the woman's two young children walking to the school bus stop. Another day, she had spotted the brother of Mr. Wilkins gathering mail, and swore that the two looked identical. It had scared her so much that she avoided the area for a couple of days after. But then her preoccupation with the murder returned with a vengeance. For the next two weeks, just about every conversation encompassed the goings-on at 221 Mulberry Drive, and Sean had just about had it.

He had been relieved when her focus shifted back to house duties. Yet, only a few days of peace later, here he was again, this time having to listen to minute-by-minute updates on the psychological collapse of a woman he once loved. Unlike his wife, he pitied her and quietly mourned the loss of her parents. He had been fond of them and was sorry for the way they had died, and he imagined that anyone in that situation could easily have ended up like Shirley, even him, had fate so chosen. He had come to believe that most people were only one tragedy separated from the nuthouse.

One evening, the two sat down to a dinner of mashed potatoes and corned beef, served with freshly baked rolls and green beans. Despite her shortcomings, Susie knew her way around the kitchen and could whip up a delectable dinner on the spot. Typically, Sean would have eaten the meal in just a few minutes, but the stench of formaldehyde from his anatomy lab lingered in his nose and overpowered the smell of the food. He had spent the afternoon using sewing pins to label tissues on a cadaver, and at one point, bodily fluids had sprayed up towards him, striking him on the shirt.

"Aren't you hungry?" Susie asked, noticing that he had barely touched his plate.

"I just need some water." He got up and walked to the sink. "Say, how did your lunch go with your mom?"

"Oh, just fine. We ate at the little seafood restaurant in town. I'm always forgetting its name."

"Johnny's Fish Shack, I think. You know, she could always stay here instead of at the hotel." But in all honesty, he was glad she was not staying with them. She was a bit pretentious for his liking and made sure everyone around was aware of her social standing. Her incessant referrals to life as the wife of Senator Wellington was enough to bore anyone.

"Yes, that's it. She's happy doing her own thing. She's been staying with friends in Seattle."

He felt relieved and managed to swallow a bite of dinner. Jackie's week-long visit was nearly over, and so far, he had managed to avoid crossing paths with her.

"Oh, did I tell you that Abby called today? You'll never believe what she said."

Sean felt his right hand tremor, an automatic and uncontrollable response to Susie's incessant gossiping that he had never experienced until a month ago, and with a loud clank, his fork hit his dinner plate. Susie seemed to take no notice.

"Well, she told me that there was so much blood that the sorority had to call in a professional cleaner. Can you just imagine?"

"Do you mind if we talk about something else, at least while we're eating?" He suddenly felt chills. Sweat began to bead on his forehead, and he held his right hand tightly with his left, suppressing the shakes.

"Oh, I'm sorry. How was lab this afternoon?" Susie asked between bites.

"Alright, I guess."

He looked down at his shirt, realizing that he had forgotten to change it after coming home. The liquid had landed right between either side of his lab coat, as if the cadaver had been aiming at his heart. He felt dizzy, nauseated. All he could smell was the formaldehyde, and all he could see was the body, its skin flayed off and tissues exposed. Suddenly, the mashed potatoes looked like fat tissue, and the corned beef looked like cadaver muscle. His head was spinning.

"What is that?" she asked, leaning towards him to take a better look. Before he could stop her, she had stuck out her finger and touched the stain. "I'm sure a little bleach…"

Before she could finish, he felt himself gag, and the table, beautifully set with dishes and crystal they had received for their wedding, was covered in everything he had eaten that day.

Susie jumped back, but it was too late. She was covered in it, too. She let out a scream and ran off towards the bathroom, horrified to find that the hairdo she had gotten with her mother that afternoon was ruined. It would be the last time she brought up Shirley's accident.

"Good morning, Ms. Fitzpatrick. I am Dr. Carl Richter, chief psychiatrist at Chastain Park Psychiatric Hospital."

A gentleman close in age to her parents sat in a chair at the other end of the room. He wore a grey, pinstripe suit over a vest and tie, the collar of his white shirt freshly starched. A white mustache topped his upper lip, a shade lighter than his silver hair. He adjusted his bifocals as he flipped through a stack of paperwork.

"Good morning." Shirley pulled her covers up towards her neck. She did not recognize the room; its lime-green walls different than what she remembered from the night before. Besides a small dresser, two metal-frame beds, the other of which sat empty, and an uncomfortable-looking wooden chair, the room was devoid of any decorative attempt. It may as well have been a prison. An ordinary black and white standard clock hung over the doorway.

"You were asleep last night when you arrived," he said, noticing her bewilderment. "Before you left Pennsylvania Hospital, did anyone explain to you where you were going?"

"Why, no. Just that I would be sent to a mental health facility for a short time…until I was better. Where am I again?" Shirley looked out the window through the bars that separated her from the outside world. She had the sudden realization that they were meant to keep her in, not to keep others out.

"This is Chastain Park Psychiatric Hospital," he repeated, "one of the finest institutions in the Commonwealth. I think you will find that we are like a large family here."

"Do they all get better…your patients?"

"A large number of them do," he said optimistically, jotting something down. He adjusted his bifocals a few more times as he wrote, and Shirley wondered whether it was a nervous habit of sorts. "Do you know why you are here?"

"I believe so." She looked down at her wrists, still wrapped in gauze and aching. It surprised her that she had slept so soundly that she had missed the transfer from the hospital entirely, especially given the pain.

"You nearly died. You are very lucky to have survived such a large amount of blood loss. Many are not so fortunate. Nonetheless, you have a serious psychiatric condition that requires treatment with the utmost urgency, and this is just the place for it. We have the best staff within these walls," he said reassuringly.

"Doctor, how long will I be here? I mean, I've got school and an internship and…" Her voice trailed off. There was the lingering burden of managing her parents' estate. The house would have to be sold, as well as her father's business. She started to say that she did not have time to be hospitalized when Dr. Richter interrupted.

"Your tasks and obligations will be there for you later on. That I can promise you." He looked at her sternly, as if evaluating whether he had made his point. Shirley nodded in acknowledgment, and he continued. "But I would surmise a couple of weeks, perhaps a little longer. It is difficult to say until we can evaluate how quickly you respond to treatment. Do you recall any of the events of yesterday evening?"

"No." She paused for a minute, carefully thinking back to the night prior. "I fell asleep there and woke up here."

"You had an episode, a psychotic episode. I am told that you even bit a nurse. You had to be sedated before you could be transferred."

Shirley looked at him, horrified. Surely, he must be mistaken.

"Bit a nurse?" she repeated back, certain she had misheard.

"I'm afraid so. The transfer notes here," he paused, looking down at his papers, "state that you became agitated for no apparent reason and lashed out at staff, ultimately biting the arm of a nurse who tried to calm you. Do you remember what transgressed prior to the event…in other words, what set it off?"

"Well, to be quite honest, I have no recollection of it at all."

Dr. Richter could see the confusion and concern in her eyes. He jotted down a few more notes.

"It is common to forget the specifics of traumatic events. The mind forgets that which it does not want to remember. It is nothing to worry about."

"Nothing to worry about? I bit someone." Shirley was humiliated. Never in her life had she done something so horrendous.

"All the more reason why you are in the right place, my dear." He straightened his back and adjusted his glasses, studying Shirley for a second before continuing. "At Chastain Park, we follow a tight schedule. There is no room for laziness or stubbornness. Breakfast is served at six, lunch at one, and dinner at seven. Weekdays rotate between therapy sessions and industry production, to which you will be assigned duties based on your skill set. I think you will find weekends to be relatively peaceful, on the contrary, resigned to card games, family visits, and outings to the therapy gardens, which are actually quite lovely this time of year.”

The door opened, and a hulking woman in traditional nursing attire emerged, a silver tray in one hand that looked miniscule by comparison.

“I’m sorry to interrupt, Dr. Richter, but it is time for Ms. Fitzpatrick’s medications.”

“We have a psychotherapy session scheduled for tomorrow at two. We will talk then.” He turned towards the nurse. “May I have a word with you?”

The nurse set down the tray at the foot of the bed and followed obediently out the door. They talked in hushed tones for a minute or two, their voices audible but words indistinguishable. Shirley looked over the covers at the contents of the tray. Two cups, no bigger than an ounce, held pills of various sizes and colors. There was a small white pill, a large gray pill, covered in dark spots, two brownish tablets, identical in appearance, and a shiny green capsule. She wondered what these mystery medications were.

The nurse reentered, this time without the doctor, holding a cup of water. Her dark, graying hair was pulled back into a nurse cap, and her white dress hung just below the knee, revealing white stockings and matching low-heeled shoes.

“Good morning. My name is Cynthia,” she introduced herself. “I will be your nurse for the day and, likely, the majority of your stay. Take these,” she commanded, handing the first cup of pills over. Her face was stern, her eyes cold and dark, and as she leaned over, the scent of cigarette smoke and cleaning solution smacked Shirley in the face, causing her to cough.

“What are these?” she heard herself ask, against her better judgment.

"Just a few medications Dr. Richter would like for you to take. They're to calm your nerves, you might say."

She swallowed as instructed.

"And these?" she wondered aloud, looking at the brown tablets and green capsule.

This time, there was no answer, just a cold glare, and Shirley quickly swallowed the next set. It was obvious Cynthia did not appreciate being asked a second time about the medications. She would just have to wait to speak to Dr. Richter again to find out. There was a harshness about the woman, a detachment, one might say, and something else that Shirley could not quite put her finger on that made her feel uneasy.

"You will have a strict schedule while you are here." She pulled a folded paper from her pocket and handed it to Shirley. "You will find your days to be quite busy, I'm sure. Dr. Richter permitted you to sleep through breakfast this morning only because of the medications you were given last night, but do not expect such luxury going forward. Lunch will be served at one o'clock sharp. You are to meet at the end of the hallway five minutes till, and together, you and the others will walk accompanied down to the dining hall."

"Others?"

"Yes, you didn't think you were the only one here, did you?" she scoffed.

"No, of course not. It's just…may I leave the room to walk around the halls?"

"With permission, yes."

"May I make phone calls?"

"The phones are off limits, I'm afraid, although we allow family visits on Sundays," she said, the edges of her lips turning up ever so slightly.

Surely, she knew. She had to know. But perhaps she did not. After the nurse left the room, Shirley inched her way to the side of the bed. The floor felt like ice against her bare feet, and her body felt weak. She held onto the foot of the bed for stability and looked out the barred window to the grassy fields beyond. It looked peaceful. She could see cattle and sheep in the distance, as well as the remnants of a corn field and what looked to be an apple orchard. Snow flurries flew past the window and onto the ground below, forming a thin layer of white. Voices carried up towards her, and she watched as several men walked towards the hospital carrying armloads of wood.

She carefully inched her way back to the bed. It was almost Christmas. She could not remember exactly which day it was, but it no longer mattered. There was no one left to celebrate with, no home to return to. Her only loved ones were at the Oakwood Cemetery, buried below six feet of soil.

Shirley had loved being an only child until now. Her parents had doted on her from the moment she was born, buying her any toys she showed the slightest interest in when walking through downtown and throwing lavish birthday parties that could rival royalty. The Fitzpatricks considered Shirley their miracle baby, having been told by doctors after years of infertility that children were not a medical possibility. There were no aunts, no uncles, no cousins, just her family of three, and it had never bothered her until her parents passed away. For the first time in her life, she noticed the absence of extended family and mourned the fact that she had no siblings. If her roommate, Cheryl, lost her parents, she would still have four sisters and a brother left. Or if Bonnie lost hers, she would at least have ten cousins to help fill the voids created by their passing. But not her. She was as alone as it gets. She wiped the dampness from her cheek and for a moment…just a split second…felt the presence of her mother beside her, perhaps even the faint feeling of an arm around her backside. And just as quickly, whatever it was that she felt vanished, and a knock came from the door.

"Ms. Fitzpatrick?" An older woman wearing nursing attire identical to Cynthia's emerged from the doorway. "I'm Geraldine from admissions. We have paperwork that needs to be completed downstairs." She looked Shirley up and down, evaluating. She was a sight to behold. The nightgown Cheryl had brought her a few days prior badly needed washing, and the bottom hem did not even hit her knees. Her hair had matted in the back from a lack of brushing. "Right this way."

"I can't possibly go about like this." Shirley looked down modestly at her attire.

"Oh, no. No, you can't." She looked at Shirley for a second before walking over to the dresser and opening the top drawer. "You'll need to change. Size?"

"Six."

She dug through the drawer for a moment before pulling out a cotton, black dress and tossing it onto the bed. "You'll find others of the same size within the top drawer." She motioned with her hand to a drawer full of identical dresses, each dark and dreary, no more cheerful than a cloudy day.

"Why are they all black?"

"We're not a fashion house. We're an asylum." Geraldine crossed her arms firmly. "I will step out while you change. Come to the door when you are done."

She left the room, closing the door behind her. Shirley held up the plain dress that was longer than her and surely would drag on the ground and after slipping it over her head, found that she was right. The long sleeves traversed her wrists and hung uncomfortably over her fingers. Only the middle fit. She knew she could alter it if she had a sewing machine, but surely, needles in an asylum were out of the question.

A few minutes later, Geraldine returned with a pair of black lace-up shoes, which were far too large, like the dress which swallowed Shirley's feet somewhere within. "I guess this will just have to do," she said with a sigh and instructed Shirley to follow.

Together, they walked down a corridor. A woman in identical black garb sat in a simple wooden chair, staring off into space, daydreaming perhaps. A few doors down, another rocked back and forth, talking to someone unseen who apparently had a sense of humor. Every few seconds, another burst of irrational laughter filled the hallway, as if she was the lucky recipient of some unheard joke. She looked at Shirley curiously, evaluating the new woman on the block with careful scrutiny, before letting out a shrill scream that could have broken a crystal glass, had one been present. Shirley jumped back.

"Don't let her scare you. She's harmless." Geraldine insisted. "Millie, another outburst like that, and I will inform Dr. Richter," she threatened, casting her a stern look, and the woman slunk cowardly back to the confines of her room.

A ring of keys emerged from her pocket. It took Geraldine a moment to unlock the heavy, double doors, which barriered off the hallway from the remainder of the hospital. When they finally did open, they moved slowly and with a loud creak, and then they quickly slammed behind them with a bang. Geraldine locked the doors and shook the handle to make sure they did not budge. Across the hall sat an identical set of doors, and she noticed Shirley looking in their direction.

"Those are the men's quarters. You are not to enter that hallway or the one directly below. Women's quarters are reserved for the other side of the hospital."

"Do you mind if I ask why?"

She gave Shirley a look, as if the question was so obvious that to ask was absurd.

"Pregnancies. We don't want pregnancies," she answered bluntly.

"Oh, I see," Shirley replied, embarrassed that the thought had not even crossed her mind. Of course, they would keep the men and women separated, she scolded herself. How could they not?

They continued their walk through the body of the hospital in what Geraldine described as the "acute" hospital floor. Patients were treated here only for medical crises, such as heart attacks or suicide attempts. It was empty that day. The lights were dim and the nurses' station quiet. Either side sat flanked by double doors identical to the ones behind them, and she explained that overnight staff beds occupied one side, with a large dining hall below, while the other side served as an overflow to the acute floor should more rooms become necessary. The hospital layout resembled a large letter H, with its double corridors branching out on each side of a centralized body. She led Shirley towards the overflow hall and down a staircase to administration below.

"You may sit in either one." Geraldine gestured towards two nicely upholstered chairs of far better quality than the one in her room. After signing initial paperwork agreeing to admission and treatment, another folder and stack of forms was presented to Shirley. "Now, I have some papers that I encourage you to sign. They serve not as a legal agreement but as a contract of goodwill between Chastain Park and you, whereby you agree to follow a few basic rules while here for your own safety and recovery. We find that patients are more likely to comply and, in turn, recover when they have agreed to certain standards in writing. You are welcome to read them in detail if you wish, but I can tell you summarily that they simply foster a shared understanding of what is expected while you are here. The rules are as follows: Number one, you must take your medications as prescribed. Number two, you must attend psychotherapy sessions as scheduled. Number three, you must never attempt to escape, as some of our past patients have tried to their detriment. Number four, you must avoid the men's quarters for reasons we discussed earlier. And number five, you are required to adhere to a strict eight o'clock bedtime. If you acknowledge and agree to abide by these rules, simply sign here…" She pointed to a black line at the bottom of a page. "Here…and here," she said, flipping to additional pages, all coated with tiny black print.

Shirley did as instructed, having no reason to doubt what she was being told. Besides, the walk to the administration hall had zapped the last of her energy, and the thought of reading through pages of instructions made her woozy.

"I want to impress upon you the importance of adhering to our…agreement. Should you, God forbid, attempt to escape or enter the men's quarters, for example, we would be forced to move you to solitary confinement, a punishment you agreed to on page three. Further, your therapy sessions would be increased and your length of stay would follow suit. I don't mean to frighten you, Ms. Fitzpatrick, only to iterate the importance of compliance. See, without compliance, there is no healing."

She pulled the paperwork towards her, stuffing it away into a file folder that she promptly walked over to a locked file cabinet.

"Well, you can rest assured that I am not planning an escape, at least not yet," Shirley laughed, hoping to lighten the mood. But the nurse did not seem to find the joke funny.

"You are very sick, my dear. Do not jest about such things. Chastain Park is amongst the finest psychiatric hospitals in the region, and I am quite confident you will find healing here, if you give it a chance, that is. It sits on nearly twelve hundred acres and produces its own food with little support from the outside world. We engage in baking, sewing, shoe making, butchering, mattress making, and art creations. Not only can we help you develop industry skills, but we can also help you earn a little money to make getting back on your feet after discharge is easier. Our goal is to foster a return to proper society, though it may take time and not always be easy." She abruptly stood up. "Follow me. We have a couple more rooms to see before lunch."

Geraldine led the way, out of the administrative hallway and into a large gathering room, the walls and wainscotting painted a bright white and far finer than the lime-green color upstairs. Comfortable-looking couches and chairs sat in little groups beneath crystal chandeliers.

"How beautiful."

"This is where patients meet with visitors on weekends and are occasionally permitted to gather. Lovely, isn't it?"

Shirley quietly nodded, once again reminded that she most likely would have no one coming to see her. The adjoining therapy room housed several small classes of special needs patients, and beyond was a therapy pool surrounded by thick humidity that created an opaque white against the windows resembling snow. Four men had just stepped out and were in the process of drying off. Several hand weights sat along the pool edge, still dripping, drawing glassy puddles around them. Geraldine noticed the glance of one of the men in Shirley's direction.

"Follow me," she ordered, leading Shirley back towards the administrative hall, across from which was the dining hall, already filled with chatter and the clanking of metal against porcelain. "You may sit where you like," she instructed before leaving Shirley alone in a room full of strangers.

Shirley sat next to one of the women she had seen in her hall that morning. Her lost glare had not changed, and Shirley wondered whether she even knew where she was.

"I'm Shirley." She stuck her hand out in introduction. The woman did not move an inch. Even her eyes stayed put, focused on a corner of the ceiling.

"Don't take it personally," a voice with a Southern drawl called out from one table over. "Maggie never responds. She's lost in her own little world."

Shirley turned to see another woman dressed in black, young and about the same age as her. Her long, red hair stood out against the darkness of the clothing, the two seeming to contradict each other like sunshine on a stormy day.

"I'm Regina," she introduced herself.

"Shirley."

"You're new here, aren't you?" She studied Shirley as if taking her in and filing her away into a category. She did not seem to be mentally handicapped or insane. Perhaps she was an epileptic, like some of the other patients who seemed relatively normal. Then she noticed the heavily bandaged wrists. She had almost missed them at first and would have were it not for the fact that Shirley rolled up her long sleeves in order to eat. Regina quickly transferred her new friend from the epileptic to the insane mental folder, though in reality, it made little difference. They were all prisoners of the ward.

"Yes. I arrived last night."

"Oh, so you're the…" She stopped short.

"The what?"

"Never mind." Suddenly, the puzzle pieces were connected. Regina had overheard the nurses discussing a new female patient who had nearly died after cutting herself. If it had not been for several blood transfusions, she never would have survived. She had also heard that the family of the new mystery patient had been lost in that American Airlines crash a few months back.

A nurse plopped a tray of food before her. Mashed potatoes, beef, and cooked carrots, with a half pint of milk on the side. She ate ravenously, having had nothing since the afternoon before. In her deep state of hunger, the food tasted almost as good as what her mom used to cook, and it was the most she had eaten since that fateful evening in October. Afterwards, her belly felt uncomfortably full, as if it had forgotten how to digest a big meal, and it would be the next morning before she would attempt another bite.

Chapter Five

The snow that had begun to fall in soft layers the day before now formed a thick, white blanket over the landscape, creating a pale canvas that drowned out the last of fall browns and oranges. Snow drifts pushed against tree trunks and hugged branches, creating the illusion of giant snow monsters along the property. Cars, left out from the day before, sat buried, barely distinguishable from one another. There was perfect stillness, a silence that might catch one off guard if unprepared for it. The small hand of the clock was just reaching six, and the sun had yet to rise. Still, light from the moon and stars bounced off the milky whiteness, forming a dusk-like ambiance that enveloped Chastain Park.

Winter had been Shirley's favorite season as a child. She and her parents often skied at the nearby slopes, and she had the fondest memories of drinking hot chocolate and apple cider at the lodge. Christmas had traditionally been a big ta-do with holiday parties, Janet's skilled gift bartering, and baking old family recipes. Was it almost Christmas already? The administrative paperwork that she had signed the day before had all been dated the eighteenth of December. Yes, almost. But it would never truly be Christmas again…not really. The plane crash had left her only with memories of a holiday she no longer knew how to celebrate.

She slipped off her nightgown and into the black "uniform." A few minutes before, a voice over the intercom had announced that it was time for morning medications and breakfast. She was already dressed when the knock came at the door. Nurse Cynthia walked right in, not waiting for a response. She looked exactly as she had the day before, her white nurse's dress and cap freshly starched and matching her stockings and shoes. She carried a tray of medications in one hand and bandages in another and quickly changed the dressings on Shirley's wrists. The wounds looked better, but they were still red and swollen. Small, black stitches remained on the right wrist where the cuts had been particularly deep.

"See to it that you cover the gauze while bathing," she reminded Shirley, holding up the saran wrap she had supplied the day prior. She reminded her that water or soap on the wound would prolong healing and possibly lead to infection. "Take these pills." She watched Shirley intently, evaluating whether she would be the type to make work easy or difficult for her. Cynthia had a stern, demanding voice and a large size that one dared not question.

She handed Shirley a cup of water and the small white pill. Then came the large gray, spotted pill, followed by the twin brown tablets, the shiny green capsule, and a new blue pill. Shirley took them as instructed. They were to calm her nerves, she had been told. She did feel a little less anxious than the day prior. Perhaps they were helping.

"Where is the schedule I provided you with yesterday?"

"On the dresser." Shirley pointed in its direction.

"See to it that you study it. I will not have a patient who cannot follow directions. You are to be punctual. Tardiness and insubordination will not be tolerated." She walked over to the dresser, picked up the schedule, and handed it to Shirley. She towered a good half foot over her. "You will meet with Dr. Richter this afternoon at two o'clock sharp. His office is down the hall and to the right. This way, please."

She led Shirley to the heavy double doors where a crowd of hungry hallmates waited to be led down to breakfast. She appeared to count the women and, after finding the number around her satisfactory and making eye contact with two other nurse chaperones, unlocked the doors.

The cafeteria bustled with activity. The women scrambled for tables, and Shirley could see that the cliques at Chastain Park were alive and well. If not for the locked doors, bars over the windows, and black uniforms, one might assume it was a casual gathering of women at a restaurant, discussing the latest fads, hairstyles, and, of course, the new girl. Shirley listened in for a moment as three women spoke in hushed tones about her, careful not to look her way, except for one, who could not help but glance her direction from time to time. It reminded her of the time someone put gum in her hair back in middle school, and the whole class snickered in amusement. She reckoned that the lack of excitement in the facility had made these women desperate for gossip.

"Oh, don't mind them." Shirley recognized the red hair first. It stood out like a sore thumb against the plainness of the uniform. "Those women are the craziest of the bunch," she laughed, sitting down across the table.

"Hi…Regina, isn't it?"

She shook her head in the affirmative. No one else had bothered to sit with Shirley. They had crammed into other tables, as if the new girl had some horrid disease that they were trying desperately to avoid. Shirley studied the brave woman before her. It was the first time she had really looked at her head-on. Her face was sprinkled with youthful freckles, her eyes a pale brown. One of her front teeth was missing, reminding Shirley of her former pupil, Julia, though the maturity of her voice and tall height stood out in stark contrast. The woman of blatant contradictions intrigued her.

"You'll have to excuse me," Shirley said, suddenly realizing that she had been staring. "I'm sorry."

"It's okay. Everyone does."

"What happened, if you don't mind my asking?" Shirley asked, pointing towards her own mouth.

"My tooth, you mean?" Regina asked, touching the gap.

"Yes."

"Oh, it was just an accident. Back when we lived in Georgia, my brother Barry and I were playing ball in the backyard with a group of neighborhood kids. Mama always warned me not to play those sorts of games…told me I'd hurt myself, give myself a black eye…so we waited until she went to the store." Well, Barry pitched, and as I swung, the ball hit me straight in the mouth. Oh, was Mama livid when she got home," she laughed.

"I can't imagine why." Shirley chuckled. It was the first time she had been able to laugh at anything since that awful day.

"Barry felt terrible about it, but it's no big deal. I kind of like it," she flashed a wide grin. When it happened, she had felt self-conscious for a while but hardly even noticed the absence these days. Regina glanced towards the three women a few tables over, who were now gleefully discussing some other topic of interest. Shirley followed her gaze.

"Who are they?"

Regina lowered her voice to a little higher than a whisper, not wanting to be overheard. "They're witches."

Shirley nearly spit out the lemonade she was drinking and had to quickly set the cup down to prevent spilling it.

"You're joking, right?"

Regina solemnly confirmed that she was not, that these women were indeed witches and were not to be messed with.

"The one on the left with the brown hair," she quickly reverted her eyesight, "is Thelma. She is in charge of the group and makes all of the decisions. Across from her are June, the one closest to the wall, and Pearl, the one closest to us."

June had short, strawberry blonde hair, neatly curled at the ends and finished with a ribbon. Pearl appeared to be the youngest of the three, no more than eighteen, with short, dark hair tied into a sloppy ponytail.

"How do you know they're witches?"

"Pearl once told me they're part of some coven. She claims they have powers and have killed several people. That's probably why they're here, if you ask me," Regina said under her breath.

"Killed people?" Even if it was not true, the mere fact that someone would talk about such a thing made her shudder. "Well, suppose they're just making it all up…for attention, maybe?"

"And end up in here? I would have just as easily kept my mouth closed."

"Have they done any witchcraft here?" Although she did not believe in witchcraft, she was, nonetheless, curious.

"Shhh, keep your voice down," Regina scolded. The word 'witchcraft' had carried a little too loudly, and she looked visibly relieved when the women did not look up from their conversation.

"Calm down. It's not as though they can really do anything."

"Oh, but they can," Regina insisted.

"What do you mean?"

"Notice how Pearl's hair is a big ol' mess? Well, it used to be long and gorgeous and the envy of the other women. About two months ago, Pearl had a roommate by the name of Willa Adams. At some point, the two got into an argument of some sort that must have upset Willa something awful. She waited until nighttime, when there were only one or two nurses on the floor, and must have unlocked the closet where the medical supplies were kept. She cut off Pearl's hair while she slept."

Shirley gasped.

"The next morning, there was a loud scream coming from their room. Several nurses ran in and found Pearl crying on the floor, running her hand through her hair, trying to tell them that someone had ruined her." Regina rolled her eyes. "Willa never admitted to it, but everyone knew. After that, Pearl got very quiet. She only talked to Thelma and June. The three of them would sit together in the hallway, murmuring what sounded like incantations, although no one could really make out what they were saying. But then, things started to happen…to Willa. She began to find clumps of her own hair on her pillow, in her brush, and on her clothes. Doctors had her tested for everything from vitamin deficiencies to anemia, but she was as healthy as an ox. She covered her head in a hat, but everyone could see that she was balding."

"That's horrible. So, what happened to her? Is she still here?"

"No, I'm afraid the story does not end happily. Unable to find answers from doctors, she became convinced that she was being poisoned. She stopped eating and drinking, except when a trusted family member brought her food on Sundays. She didn't sleep, didn't shower. And then, one morning, they found her dead in her bed. She died in her sleep, they told us, though no one believed that for a second. Oh, it was horrible. Absolutely awful. I saw her mother come to collect her things one morning, and I couldn't bear to look at her, the poor woman."

Shirley grabbed a tissue from her pocket and wiped the tear from her cheek. Her reaction to the story of Willa caught her by surprise.

"Oh, goodness. Whatever is the matter?"

"I'm sorry." She paused, sniffled, and wiped her nose with the tissue. "It's just such a sad story." But the truth of it was that that was not it at all. She cried for herself. For the first time, she felt sorry for herself, really sorry. Sorry that she had no mother to love her and never would again. Sorry, too, that she would never have family to visit her on Sundays. It was gone…all of it. Every ounce of anything that had been of importance to her was gone…her parents, her fiancé, and most certainly her teaching offer, once they found out she was in the looney bin. After all, who would want their child to be taught by a teacher deemed mentally unstable?

"Well, I wouldn't feel too sorry for Willa. Rumor has it that the reason she was even here to begin with is that she murdered her infant son."

"Oh, how awful. Why wasn't she in prison?"

"Because she was found to be insane, like the rest of us." She gestured around the room. "Word of advice…watch your back here, and you'll be fine."

The witches had finished eating and were just exiting the doors when Shirley happened to catch June looking her way. There did not seem to be anything strange about her. If anything, she looked lovely, a Grace Kelly-type of natural beauty that evoked a sense of trust, quite the counterpart to what one would consider a witch. There was a familiarity about her that Shirley could not place. The two women studied each other for a moment, their gaze only broken by a kick on the shin from Regina.

Dr. Richter's office was nothing more than a large closet with a window. It housed a bookcase filled with psychiatric literature that one might expect a physician to consult on occasion. *Personality*, *The Meaning of Anxiety*, and *Psychiatric Social Work* sat in a stack on one of the chairs to the right. A torn newspaper clipping sat wedged deep within the first, marking a page of supposed relevance. On the other side of the room was a loveseat and an adjacent four-foot-tall spruce, decorated with small ornaments and silver streamers. The room smelled like fresh pine, a pleasant change from the stench of cigarette smoke and body odor that encompassed the rest of the facility. Shirley sat down and glanced at the clock above the door. It was five after two. Dr. Richter would be there any minute, the nurse had promised five minutes before.

Out the window was the gray bleakness of a late fall afternoon. The sun had retired and would remain hidden for the next few months. Daylight resembled more of a twilight, and if not for the reflection of light off the snow, it would have been almost dark already. Christmas was only a few days away now. She imagined her sorority sisters all home for the holidays, listening to Christmas music, visiting the local ice rinks, running last-minute errands…all the things she would miss this year.

At last, the door opened, and Shirley stood back up. Dr. Richter was wearing a gray suit over a bluish vest with a festive red tie covered in tiny Santa Clauses, each carrying a large bag of gifts over his backside. His mustache was neatly trimmed, his grayish-white hair slicked into a deep side part.

"Good afternoon, Ms. Fitzpatrick. My apologies for keeping you waiting. Please sit back down. There is no need for formalities here."

"Good afternoon, doctor," she said, returning to her seat.

He moved the book pile to the floor and sat down, a folder, pen, and small notebook in hand. He glanced through the contents of the folder for a few seconds before speaking.

"How are you settling in?"

"Quite well, I suppose."

"Any side effects from the medications, like nausea, dizziness, or excessive tiredness?"

"No, I don't believe so. But I'd like to know which medications I'm receiving. Nurse Cynthia seems unwilling to tell me."

The doctor adjusted his bifocals and, without looking up, answered, "They are my proprietary combination of psychotropic agents to help with anxiety and depression. You may find that it takes several weeks before any benefit is seen, and we may adjust dosage along the way to get it just right."

"Well, I'm hoping I won't be here that long. I'm feeling much better now."

"I wish it was as simple as feeling better, my dear, but these things take time, and you will have to be patient. You nearly perished," he reminded her. "There is no rushing the process."

"I understand, but you see, I have a great deal of matters to attend to at the moment," she reminded him.

"You are still quite ill, I can assure you. Your place, for the moment, is here. Outside duties and obligations will be there waiting for you once you recover."

Shirley detected a look of subtle annoyance on his face at having to reiterate the point. She decided not to press the issue. Perhaps he was right. After all, she had nearly died back in the sorority house.

"What sort of skills do you have?" Dr. Richter asked, looking up.

"Skills?"

"Yes. Do you sew, bake, garden, paint, or have any experience in the areas of butchering, mattress making, or shoe repair?" He doubted the latter three, given her upbringing and social status, but thought he would ask, nonetheless, given the growing difficulty finding anyone with such abilities. Geraldine had mentioned the industry side of Chastain Park the day prior, and she had had a night to ponder the tasks she would take on.

"Oh, yes, of course. I'm afraid I'm not a painter and have never worked with mattresses or shoes, but I do bake quite often and have experience gardening."

"Very good. Francis Hall sits on the other side of the therapy gardens. You will spend Tuesdays and Thursdays baking a variety of items to be sold. Depending on how long you stay, you may eventually help with the gardening as well."

The thought of being at the asylum in the spring was so outlandish that she laughed at the mere possibility. Dr. Richter seemed not to share in her amusement. There was something he was turning over in his mind. He opened his mouth as if to speak, then closed it, evaluating the words he wished to say one last time before letting them float off into the air.

"I was told by Nurse Geraldine that I would earn a portion of the proceeds?"

"Yes, that's correct. Twenty percent of the earnings will be set aside and given to you upon your discharge. I see here," he said, flipping through his notes, "that you agreed to Chastain Park's rules agreement yesterday. Do you have any questions about what is expected of you while you're a patient?"

"No."

"Very well then. Now that we have the necessities accounted for, I'd like for us to talk about you…and the family you so tragically lost. In recent years, psychotherapy has blossomed, if you will, into a quite effective method of curing what ails the mind. For you, it would mean conversing and delving deep into the psyche to find out what makes it tick…and what derails it."

She had never talked to a psychiatrist in her life, and she did not know anyone else who had, or who would admit to it anyway. There was a stigma around such a thing, and you could become a pariah should a mental health struggle be discovered.

"Tell me about your parents. What were they like? What did you do together as a family?"

Shirley took a deep breath. It had been nearly two months, but it had not gotten any easier to talk about what happened…or them. If she blocked it out, she could pretend everything was normal. But for the first time since their deaths, she was being put on the spot and *had* to talk about it. She could not hide. The air sat in her lungs, unwilling to pass through her vocal cords. Dr. Richter put his hand on her knee.

"It's okay. When you're ready. Just take your time."

She grabbed a tissue and dabbed her eyes, glad that she was not wearing makeup.

"I'm sorry." She took a deep breath. "My dad…Bill…he was a businessman. He owned several furniture stores on the East Coast. He loved to fish. He often took me with him as a little girl to various lakes, and we caught trout and bass that mom would cook up. The Yankees were his favorite. We drove to New York several times to see them play. I guess you could say I had to fill the position of the son he never got."

Though it had been years since they had made a fishing trip, memories of wading into shallow waters with a fishing pole stuck fresh in her mind, as if it happened yesterday. Baseball hats and other memorabilia acquired over the years took up an entire shelf of her old bedroom closet. The reminder that there would be no more fishing trips or baseball games suddenly stuck her like a knife in the gut. Dr. Richter jotted down something and patiently waited for her to continue.

"My mother's name was Janet. She loved to cook and garden, founded a poetry club at the local library, and was very active in her church. We did everything together." The sole tissue was her security blanket, and she clutched it for dear life. "They were great, both of them," she sniffed.

Dr. Richter smiled in acknowledgment. "It sounds like a close-knit family." She nodded, wiping another tear with the tissue that now resembled a small ball.

"Walk me through how you have coped with the tragedy. What strategies have you developed that have worked, and what has not?"

But Shirley did not hear him. Only the sound of a strange hissing met her ears, soft at first and then growing louder, coming from somewhere in the room. Perhaps a heating vent was kicking on, she wondered. When she looked up, Dr. Richter was looking at her.

"I'm sorry. Did you say something?"

"I inquired about the coping mechanisms you have found helpful and unhelpful in the wake of your parents' deaths."

"I guess you could say that walking in nature has helped…and talking about them with those who knew them well. We don't have other family, but once in a while, my dad's longtime friend, Jeff, gives me a call to check-in. He's written some nice letters with stories of their friendship as children. But he's been ill himself, so I haven't spoken with him in a month now."

She heard the hiss again, this time behind her right ear and louder. She swung around quickly, but there was nothing out of the ordinary. Dr. Richter quickly jotted down another note.

"And you began cutting yourself after their deaths, is that right?"

"Yes." She looked down, somewhat embarrassed to discuss her secret outlet.

"Now, there's no need to feel ashamed," he said, noticing her reaction. "When tragedy hits us, we're all affected differently. Some people may stop eating. Some may eat too much. Others may drink or turn to drugs…and others to physical self-harm."

"I guess it started a week or so after. I didn't mean to do it. It was an accident, really, but it just continued. It's the only way I feel normal, after I cut, like all of my problems disappear for a while."

"That is because it causes a very temporary release of endorphins that may perk your mood. But it is, quite obviously, not a healthy strategy for coping. I am quite confident that our sessions, in combination with group therapy and the proper medications, will help you to manage the hardships of life more solidly. What you are dealing with is much more common than you might…"

His words trailed off as her attention was grasped by what was manifesting on the wall before her. A shadow slithered across, the gray weaving back and forth as it stretched from one side of the wall to the other, led by a forked tongue. And then, there was another. The shadow wriggled this way and that, upwards and then changing course to the left. Two more slithering shapes joined in from the side, and this continued until the wall was filled with ghostly shadows that seemed to be cast from thin air. Their hissing and rattling masked all other noise, and the office suddenly felt as though it had become a nightmarish rainforest.

"…and that is why I have arranged…" Dr. Richter suddenly stopped, noticing Shirley's wide eyes tracking something beyond him, and he quickly turned to look at whatever had grasped her attention. There was nothing, at least nothing that he could see, except for a white wall and framed diplomas showcasing his finest educational achievements. "Ms. Fitzpatrick. Ms. Fitzpatrick," he repeated, a look of concern on his face, "are you alright?"

She looked at him, then back to the wall, but the shadows were gone, vanishing just as quickly as they appeared. Even the sounds of hissing had evaporated into silence, and the room resumed its typical character, no more threatening than any other physician's office. Shirley had the rather sudden and unpleasant realization that she could not share the horror she had just experienced. If she dared mention hallucinations, she would almost certainly have another psychiatric diagnosis added to her chart, prolonging her stay even longer, perhaps forever. There was no choice but to keep quiet.

"Yes, I'm sorry. It's just been a long day, and I'm a little tired."

The doctor did not press further, though she noticed with disappointment that he jotted once again in the notebook, presumably marking the event down for further scrutiny.

"I find, in my practice, that most people tend to lose control and harm themselves when healthy coping mechanisms for stress, anxiety, depression…what have you…are not actively prioritized. Therefore, I ask that you preemptively develop and write down five appropriate coping strategies, which you may share next time." He handed Shirley a small notebook, similar to his own, blank except for fine ruling. "One strategy might be as simple as going for a walk. Another could entail writing a journal entry. We will meet again on Wednesday, two days from now, at the same time. Oh, and one more thing. I would like for you to make an effort to talk to the other women on your ward. The isolation of Chastain Park can be daunting, especially in the winter, and finding comradery with another in your shoes can be incredibly helpful."

Dr. Richter sounded optimistic. His face exuded confidence, and Shirley could see why others respected him. For the first time, Shirley felt like there was nothing to worry about, that this disorder she had developed would soon be controlled, and that life would go on as usual.

Walking back to her room, she was met with a cloud of smoke billowing from the nurses' station, where a group of four nurses huddled together, writing in charts and chitchatting about life outside the asylum, cigarettes in one hand and pens in the other. One of the ashtrays sat on the edge of the counter, full of yellowish-brown cigarette butts and ashes. The sight was almost enough to make her sick.

Shirley had always hated cigarettes. Her mother had stopped smoking when Shirley was a toddler after she ate the contents of an ashtray and became violently ill. Ever since then, even the smell was intolerable, and unlike most of her friends, she had never picked up a cigarette in her life. Strangely enough, she loved the smell of cigars, especially her father's collection of Cubans.

Her room felt like a refuge from the rest of the hospital. Little tasks like making her bed and folding her clothes made her feel at home. She had just sat down in the lone chair and entitled the first page of her notebook 'Strategies' when a knock came from the door. She put her pen down.

"Come in," she started to say when the door flung open. Nurse Cynthia walked in, carrying her usual silver medication tray, but this time followed by a young woman about Shirley's age. She had dark, tangled hair that was pulled back into a partial updo. The nurse seemed to barely notice Shirley and led the new woman over to the dresser, pulling out a dress that Shirley had just finished folding.

"You will find your clothing here. Your bed is there." She pointed to the empty bed across the room. Then, she handed her a piece of paper and, just as she had with Shirley the day before, explained, "We run a tight schedule here at Chastain Park. Your days will be busy. Medications and breakfast are at six o'clock, lunch at one, and dinner at seven. You are to meet in the hallway at five till and will walk as a group down to the dining hall. Your schedule will alternate between therapy sessions and working in the industry hall, all of which is described on there," she said, pointing to the sheet.

The new woman took her medications and started to ask a question when Cynthia abruptly walked out. Shirley giggled, reminded of her own experience with the nurse. The other woman could not help but laugh, too. There was a humor in Cynthia's strangeness that would serve as a bond between them.

The woman extended her arm. "Hi, I'm Barbara."

"Shirley."

Chapter Six

Barbara Walker was a simple girl, the type who did not require the finer things in life. In many ways, she was quite the opposite of Shirley, unruly and rough around the edges. She smoked heavily and, along with the nursing staff, created enough billowing, white clouds to set off the smoke detectors. Her unkempt hair looked as though it had never been properly tamed, and her young voice had an unexpected rasp and cracked as she spoke. Yet there was a beauty in her eyes that drew Shirley in and an empathy, as if she understood everything about you with just a glance.

Barbara moved to the beat of her own drum. It seemed that she said and did as she pleased, without regard for societal norms. She had worked as a secretary at a dental office since right after high school, finding fulfillment in her career choice, and, at the age of twenty-three, had already been married and divorced twice. Following her most recent split, she had moved to a small apartment outside of Philadelphia and had sung at dance clubs in the evenings for extra income.

Despite their differences, the two women took an immediate liking to each other. They complimented each other in just the right ways and actually shared quite a bit in common. Shirley was relieved just to have a roommate, while Barbara was thankful she seemed normal enough. In a mental health asylum, you never knew who you might be bunking with.

Barbara took a drag of her cigarette. "This one evening, several years ago," she began, "I was singing down at the Blue Bird. Have you heard of it?" The end of the cigarette tapped the tray, knocking half an inch of ash into the pile that badly needed emptying.

Shirley nodded. She had been to the club many times before, mostly with Sean and, more recently, with her roommate, Cheryl. It was a hole-in-the-wall place in downtown Philly that you had to have been shown to find. Not that it was a secret club in any way, just hidden by virtue of the fact that it was located within an old mill, the front of which was somewhat obscured by old oak trees. An inconspicuous door, marked only by a small, iron sign above it with the words 'Blue Bird' in weathered relief, was difficult to spot from the street. And just when one opened the door, expecting to have found it, the search continued. An astute visitor might notice that the bookshelf in the corner was slightly ajar, and should they choose to investigate, would find live music and dancing on the other side. They would also discover a bartender working feverishly, pouring drinks at a fascinating speed, and a cocktail waitress in a black minidress carrying drinks on a tray, mingling with guests as she delivered rum and cokes and whiskey shots. Sean had once joked that the owner was brilliant. The speakeasy-esque bar could quickly vanish behind the bookcase in the event of unpaid taxes or unwanted inspections, and no one would be the wiser.

"Well, this gentleman walks in. He wore a top hat, like so many other patrons, so at first, I didn't recognize him, but when he took it off, I realized it was James Stewart!"

"The actor from *It's a Wonderful Life*?" It was one of Shirley's favorite movies. She had watched it in the theater several times when it had been out.

"Yes, that's him. He was filming a new movie and was in town for a few weeks. A very kind man and dreamy." She exaggerated the word dreamy, and her eyes lit up thinking about him. "He asked me for my number, and we went on a few dates, but it didn't work out. I was only eighteen at the time, and he must have been close to forty. But we sure had a blast."

"I heard he has another movie with Grace Kelly coming out next year…*Back Window* or *Rear Window*…something of the sort anyway," Shirley laughed. "I'm surprised I've never run into you there…the Blue Bird, I mean."

"Odd, isn't it?" She took another long and thoughtful drag of the cigarette before enthusiastically delving into her day job at the dental office and how much stability it brought her during her divorces. She had butted heads with the office manager, a plump, older gentleman by the name of Joseph, several times over the strict attendance policy and dress code, yet somehow always managed to keep her job.

As Barbara rambled on, her words seemed to melt away, replaced by the horrifying sound of hissing. Out of the corner of her eye, something slithered near her feet, and she quickly lifted them up. Barbara hardly seemed to notice and continued on about a former coworker, who had been fired for stealing lidocaine and reselling it on the street. Another shadow slithered out from under her bed, hissing louder than the others, and then dozens more followed. The floor shifted and swayed in a sea of dark leather. It felt like Dr. Richter's office all over again. Shirley screamed, and with that, the phenomenon ceased.

"Are you alright? Whatever is the matter?" Barbara ran to her side, panicked. Something on the floor seemed to have frightened her new roommate, but as she scoured the tiles, desperately searching for something, anything, out of the ordinary, she noticed nothing amiss. It looked like any old floor that one might find in a medical facility. "What's going on?" she pleaded when Shirley did not answer.

The look of fear on Shirley's face dissipated when she realized that the snakes were indeed gone. But where to? Was it all some sort of hallucination? There was no other explanation for it. She would…she must…keep it to herself unless she wanted to end up like her aunt Catherine.

"I'm sorry. I just thought I saw a bug," she lied. "What were you saying?" she continued, somewhat embarrassed and eager to change the subject.

Barbara was not convinced. "You did not look fine a second ago."

"It's nothing," Shirley insisted. "I'm just a little tired, I guess." But it was something, and deep down, she knew it…and Barbara knew it too. Never in her life had she seen things that were not there. An uncomfortable knot formed in her stomach, one that would keep her up for much of the night.

Barbara began to fear that she had been mistaken, that she had been paired with a crazy roommate after all, although what could one expect in such a place, she reminded herself. That night, she slept with one eye open, just in case.

The sound of the six o'clock intercom jolted both women awake. "Morning meds in five minutes," repeated the voice three times. They scrambled out of their nightgowns and into twin black uniforms, removing all signs of individuality and autonomy. At exactly five past six, Cynthia emerged with a silver tray in each hand, one for Shirley, the other for Barbara. Shirley watched as she handed Barbara her medications, one by one. A small white pill, a large gray pill with dark spots, two brownish tablets, a shiny green capsule, and a spotted pink pill that she had not seen before. By the looks of her regimen, Shirley gathered that their psychiatric disorders must be quite similar.

"What are all these?" Barbara asked, just as Shirley had.

"Just some medicine to boost your mood," Cynthia begrudgingly answered, offering no further explanation. "Any further questions can be directed to Dr. Richter."

She walked across the room to Shirley and, without any pleasantries, handed the first of the medication collection over. The white and gray pills, the two brown tablets, the shiny green capsule, a blue pill, and a new one…pinkish with small, multi-colored spots. It reminded her of pink icing covered in sprinkles or a colorful jelly bean. She wanted to ask what this new one was and why it was added. Cynthia seemed prepared for the inquiry and quickly squashed any attempts to question the regimen with a preemptive scowl. Shirley quietly swallowed the pills. She would add it to her mental list of items to discuss with the doctor the following day.

The duo ate breakfast with Regina, who eagerly caught Barbara up to date on the rumored coven at Chastain Park. She kept her voice down when discussing them, fearful of being overheard.

Shirley could not help but glance at the women. Thelma and Pearl ate bacon, eggs, and toast while June nibbled on a cream cheese-covered bagel. They had their own seemingly benign conversation going, appearing no more harmful than a group of women meeting for brunch. Pearl was barely old enough to drive and still had quite a bit of baby fat in her face, making the rumor of witchcraft and fatal spell-casting almost laughable. Yet, Shirley kept her mouth shut as Regina swore that the witches had been at it again. She shared a wall with two of the women and, the night before, had apparently heard them reciting an indistinguishable prayer in tandem, only to awaken the following morning with the wall behind her headboard covered in strange drawings.

"I'm worried they're out to get me…that I'm next," she said, legitimate terror in her eyes.

"Oh, come now. Why would they want to do that?" Shirley asked gently, hoping to calm her nerves.

"Because I know too much about them, and they don't like it," she answered bluntly.

Shirley glanced over at the women once again. June met her gaze, and Shirley quickly looked away, feeling a shiver run through her body.

"I believe in witches," Barbara chimed in, lighting up a cigarette. "My stepmother was an evil woman, who I believed had my father cursed. After he filed for divorce, she became bitter and moved in with her friend, a woman who openly practiced witchcraft. Within a few weeks, his business failed, he got very sick with pneumonia, and we even had a house fire. It was just too much at once to be a coincidence."

"Why, that's terrible," Shirley replied.

"Yes. Well, it was years ago now. She died not long after that of cancer." She blew a smoke ring and smiled proudly at her skill.

"So, what are you going to do about it?" Shirley asked Regina.

"Them?" she asked, cocking her head in the direction of the witches.

Shirley nodded.

"Clean up the wall and move to the other bed, I guess. Obviously, it's not something I can tell the nurses." She twirled her long, red hair up into a bun before excusing herself. "I'm off to start my sewing. Nice to meet you, Barbara."

Shirley got up a moment later. It was her first day baking, a task for which she would make one dollar per hour, creating pastries, cookies, breads and cakes to be sold to the outside world. A group had already gathered by the entrance, waiting for the front doors to be unlocked. It was industry day, the day that the competent and able-bodied walked the short distance to Francis Hall, an old, two-story barn that had been converted into a mill of sorts, divided into sections by discipline. The loft was home to sewing, shoe and mattress making, and art creations, while the first floor was comprised of a large kitchen used for baking and butchering and, during fertile summer months, packing produce for shipment.

A staff member handed out dark coats of varying sizes, and the group departed into the six-inch-deep snow, now hard and crunchy, having melted and refrozen a few days prior, the remnants of a recent snow shower lightly dusting the top like a coat of powdered sugar. It was a slippery trap for the unsuspecting.

"Watch for ice," one of the chaperoning nurses cautioned.

Everyone walked with iron feet, not wanting to be the one who made a fool of themselves. The therapy garden sat in quiet beauty, benches partially buried and cypresses wilting beneath the weight of the snow. A round koi pond had frozen at the surface, and to the left were several large pots housing snow plants that rose up and then fell to the ground, resembling the shapes of tall grass and English ivy. There was silence, except for the crunching of snow beneath feet, breaking the pristine white coverage of the land, perfect except for small double footprints that hopped merrily about.

The barn lied just beyond, and once inside, Shirley began work in earnest on ten apple pies, eight batches of chocolate chip cookies, and five loaves of bread. It was a good start, not great but good enough for her first day, and by late afternoon, she had earned eight dollars.

It was after dinner before Shirley and Barbara returned to their rooms. Both were exhausted and barely spoke before jumping into bed. Barbara had spent the afternoon signing paperwork and meeting with a therapist, and her eyes were still red from the emotional toll of the latter. Shirley emersed herself in *A Tree Grows in Brooklyn* and read for the next few hours, occasionally distracted by the movement of something out of the corner of her eye or hissing from the far corner, but she knew enough now to understand it was not real.

She was already asleep when Cynthia entered the room to change the dressings. Her wrists were healing nicely. A physician at the prior hospital had warned her that scaring was to be expected, and she had somewhat prepared herself for the unsightly wounds. There was a sadness with the realization that short sleeves may never again be an option, unless she was willing to handle unwanted stares and possibly even questions in public.

Just before leaving, Cynthia stopped, remembering something, and reached into her pocket. "I nearly forgot. This arrived for you today." Her voice was emotionless, sterile.

She pulled out an envelope and handed it to Shirley, saying nothing further, before leaving. SHIRLEY FITZPATRICK was written in all caps on the front in the blue ink of a ballpoint pen. There was no return address. She quickly ripped the envelope open, eager to see its contents. Red flowers painted in watercolor decorated the front of the card, and inside was a note of well wishes written by several women in the sorority. "We wish you all the best and think of you every day. We cannot wait to see you when you are well. Enjoy the magazines, books, and desserts! Merry Christmas!" the note concluded.

She had not received any gifts and wondered what they meant. She peeked out her door. Cynthia was nowhere to be seen, but a group of nurses still lingered at the nurses' station, eating and smoking as they wrapped up for the evening. One in the back was already engrossed in a novel and looked up only for a second before getting back to her book.

"Excuse me," Shirley said politely, walking in their direction. "Where can I find a package that was sent to me?"

A young, blonde nurse looked up from a copy of *Ladies' Home Journal*, a cigarette dangling from her mouth like a lollipop. The look of irritation upon her face reminded her of her interactions with

Cynthia, and she wondered whether Chastain Park had some unwritten rule forbidding questions. She lowered the magazine beside a small plate of coffee cake and cookies.

"Package?" The blonde's tone insinuated that she had never heard of something so strange as a patient receiving a package. She resumed flipping through the magazine, Shirley's plight of no interest to her.

"Yes, with magazines, books, and desserts, I believe."

"I haven't the slightest of inclinations, but I will make sure to tell you should I…locate it," the blonde nurse promised, tapping her cigarette on an ashtray. There was a muffled cough that came from somewhere in the back. Shirley looked around the nurses' station. A stack of romance novels and women's magazines sat next to patient charts. A tray of cookies, decorated in icing with various Christmas designs, sat open, some half-eaten and discarded, their paper wraps littering the counter space and floor. She felt her face flush a deep red and her heart beat faster. She took a few deep breaths. It was just a coincidence. No one could be so callous. And just as she began to feel guilty for allowing her thoughts to drift to such darkness, the blonde let out a high-pitched, schoolgirl giggle and ate another cookie with exaggerated sounds of enjoyment before boastfully licking her fingers free of any leftover icing.

"Oh, Darlene," she said, addressing the brunette nurse beside her, "you have just *got* to try these cookies." The blonde took another bite.

The anger came rushing back. There was no stopping it this time. She lunged at the blonde, ripping the last half of the cookie from her hands, and slapped her across the cheek, leaving the pink outline of her hand behind. The blonde's smile melted away and into a look of shock.

"How could you?" Shirley shrieked.

The nurses sat frozen, watching the rampage before them, as Shirley grabbed as many of the magazines, books, and cookies as she could carry. Half of them dropped to the floor on the walk back to her room, but she did not care, as long as *they* were not enjoying her presents. She slammed the door behind her, just in time for the ear-piercing security alarms, and within seconds, the entire floor was in a frenzy. Dr. Richter and a team of staff members burst through the door unannounced. Barbara awoke with a start and watched in bewilderment from her bed as two male nurses administered a tranquilizer across the room. Shirley thrashed and screamed for a minute, at one point kicking a nurse in the chest and sending him flying backwards, but within seconds, her strength gave way to flaccid limbs, which were subsequently secured by four-point restraints.

"What happened?" Dr. Richter asked the blonde nurse.

"Doctor, it was as though she suddenly lost all sense of reality. She came to the nurses' station asking for a package and, when I told her I'd let her know if I came across it, she gave me a strange look and then lunged at me, like a wild animal. It was awful."

"I can only imagine. Did she happen to say anything before this occurred?"

"Not that I can recall."

The other staff returned to their duties, but the doctor and blonde remained by the door. Barbara laid back down and listened to their conversation out of curiosity. Who was this new roommate, she wondered.

In quiet tones, the doctor continued to press. "Are you certain she did not mention anything else?"

"I do not believe so."

"Did she appear to see or hear anything strange before the incident?"

"Why, no, doctor, not that I noticed." The blonde looked at him, mystified.

A few minutes later, an older nurse emerged from the hallway and sat in the lone chair of the room. Geraldine would be Shirley's sitter for the remainder of the evening.

Dr. Richter was thankful to have the night off. Dr. Abrams was the onsite physician that evening and would handle any emergencies that arose. He quickly sped away in his Buick sedan, driving a little too quickly for the icy road conditions. Mariam would be expecting him soon for dinner…and his mother, that old grouch. Ruth had moved in six months ago when her health started to decline. Prior to that, she had lived in the home he had grown up in, but a stroke over the summer had rendered her incapable of using the stairs or managing her own care without assistance.

Mariam greeted him by the front door, as she always did when he arrived home. She was a gracious woman who rarely complained, even about Ruth. Her collared dress was hidden behind a green, gingham-print apron, and she rushed inside before him to take a shortcake out of the oven. In many ways, she did not mind the extra work, now that their three boys were grown and off on their own. It brought her back to the maternal role that suited her best.

"I'll have dinner ready in five minutes."

He set his coat on a hook and slipped off his leather shoes that dripped with the remnants of snow. The table was set with their finest dishes and glassware that had been given to them nearly three decades prior as wedding gifts. For years, they had sat untouched in a china cabinet, lest one of their sons broke something. But as they progressed through middle age and friends became widows and widowers, she abandoned the notion of saving nice things for special occasions. Life was too short.

"Carl? Is that you?" came a shaky voice from the den. An older woman buried in a long sweater sat on one of the sofas. Its green knitting matched the carpet, nearly blending in.

"Yes, mother. I'm home."

"For the whole evening?"

"Yes, until tomorrow morning."

Ruth got up, her legs somewhat wobbly, and held tight to the armrest of the sofa as she steadied herself. Carl rushed to her side, afraid she would fall and injure herself, and he would end up in a hospital room with her on his night off. She held his arm as they made their slow walk to the kitchen.

"You know, Mariam upset me today," she whispered.

She was always complaining about something and every evening, it was a new story about Mariam. He was growing weary of the tattle-telling, and it was becoming harder to hide his disdain for his mother's unappreciative attitude. Had it not been Mariam, she would be in a facility, and on more than one occasion, he had nearly let that forgotten fact slip.

"This afternoon, we went to bridge with the neighborhood women. Sally Franklin started going on about the new houses her husband's company…what is it called?"

"New Dawn Homes, I believe."

"That's it. Now, what was I saying?"

"Sally's husband is building houses." Carl took a deep breath, attempting to keep his patience. He was starving. Could this not wait?

"Oh, yes. So, Sally Franklin boasted to the group about how each home costs only three thousand to produce but sells for over seven thousand and how the company built ten houses last year. Well, you can do the calculation."

"Mother, where is this going?" Carl asked, looking in the direction of the kitchen.

Ruth did not care whether her son wanted to talk right now or not. She was going to tell him exactly what happened. "Understandably, I encouraged Mariam to share all the brilliant work you're accomplishing out at Chastain Park, but your wife refused. She just about stomped on my toe when I prodded. Wouldn't even prop you up in front of her friends. You know, she's exactly like your father, too humble for her own good."

He wanted to tell her to stop it and that he was thankful Mariam had not given in to pressure, but he could never confront his mother. It would quickly lead to her crying and saying something along the lines of, "You don't care if I live or die," as she did whenever someone stood up to her. He had seen it play out many times before when his father was alive. She sat on an imagined, elevated pedestal within the galaxy of her own mind and responded angrily whenever it was threatened, protecting it by whatever means necessary from tumbling down. He was ten years old the last time he had challenged her, and he had quickly learned never to do it again.

"Dinner's ready!" called a familiar voice from the kitchen.

"How was your day?" Carl asked Mariam, grateful to change the subject.

"Lovely. I took your mother to the grocer, and then we went to the Franklin's for bridge and tea." It was quite obvious she had not overheard Ruth's ranting in the other room. She gave the older woman a warm smile, which Ruth unapologetically ignored, shuffling quickly past and over to her seat at the table.

"What's this?" Ruth asked, picking up the meatloaf with a fork, as if it was some foreign object that belonged nowhere near a plate. She slapped it back down on the table.

"Meatloaf," Mariam responded, confused. It was slightly overcooked, but anyone with a brain could tell what it was.

"It looks like that rabbit Carl hit with his car a few weeks back." She laughed like a hyena and gave her son's shoulder a nudge. Mariam was shocked at the mere referral. The rudeness of this woman. "If you wanted a good meatloaf recipe, all you had to do was ask. When Carl was growing up, I made it all the time. It was his father's favorite."

"Your father…tomorrow would have been his birthday." Mariam looked at Carl, who had inherited the elder Richter's tall, thin frame and piercing brown eyes, yet lacked his ability to keep Ruth in line. "Will you be able to join us at the cemetery? Your mother and I are planning to bring some flowers."

"I'm due back at the hospital by eight, so only if it's first thing in the morning." He took a bite of the macaroni and cheese, quickly followed by a bite of biscuit. Ruth had successfully ruined his appetite for the meatloaf, which he had scooped to the side of his plate, much to her delight.

"We can manage an early morning, can't we?" Mariam asked the old woman.

"If you say so," she answered without looking up. Mariam was quite certain that she would not visit the grave at all if it were not for her urging. In fact, Mariam had been the one to order the flowers, maintain the gravesite weekly, and ensure James Richter had any familial visitors at all.

Ruth had a coldness about her which had only worsened after becoming a widow. Mariam could not help but wonder how much of a hand her husband had had in keeping her oddities hidden. She had tried to bring it up to Carl on more than one occasion, only to be silenced. Nothing bad could be said about the woman who raised him, despite how poorly she treated everyone else. He tiptoed around her and protected her, often at the expense of his own wife, and it was starting to grate on her.

"So, it's settled then." She smiled satisfactorily, keeping her lips pressed tightly together. One day, the words would slip out, most likely by accident, but not tonight.

When Carl had announced that he was moving his mother in, Mariam had been nothing but supportive. But six months later, she felt that it was her own health that was declining. The level of care Ruth required left her with little time or energy for anything outside of the home. Nor could she leave the older woman alone due to the very real possibility that she might try to cook and burn the house down in the process. It reminded her of the days of having toddlers at home.

Ruth had moved into their eldest son's old bedroom, and Mariam had gone through great efforts to ensure it was ready for her arrival. She made a new quilt for the bed, sewed new curtains, and purchased new art for the walls, all in the dark blue that was her favorite color. Yet, it was never enough to win her over. Ruth was nasty at every intersection, and Mariam sensed that she viewed her as competition for Carl's love. It was the constant swipes, like at dinner that night, that had made Mariam feel as though she was the other woman in her own marriage. She walked past the den and grabbed her coat from the rack, announcing that she was going for a short walk and would be back soon.

"It's nearly dark. And it's cold and icy out there. You should stay home," Carl cautioned. But by the time he finished his sentence, she was already out the door and down the steps of the entryway. She did not care how cold or slippery it was. She just had to get out of that house.

Chapter Seven

Ahem. Dr. Richter cleared his throat a couple of times and ruffled through his papers. She wondered whether he ever prepared before sessions or just winged it, perhaps making things up as he went along. Finally, he landed on the page he was looking for.

"Tell me, Ms. Fitzpatrick. What happened yesterday?"

Shirley looked down. She had been in restraints since the evening before, and it was not until an hour ago that Cynthia finally removed them. Her ankles were sore and red, and the scars on her wrists throbbed, as did her back from lying in the same position for so long. Having had time to think about what transpired, she had only grown angrier and more certain that she was in the right.

"The nurses…they stole my package. They knew it was for me, and they took it anyways," she said through gritted teeth, struggling to keep her voice down. "Those things were *mine!*" She wrestled with the cushion behind her, unable to find a comfortable position.

"I understand that such an event, were it true, would be quite unsettling. Tell me, why do you believe they took your package?"

Shirley looked at Dr. Richter for a moment, thinking she must have misheard what he just said. But no, she had heard him correctly. *Were it true?* He did not believe her.

"I received a card from my sorority sisters, which said to enjoy the magazines, books, and desserts. It is reasonable to assume that a package with those items was sent to me. When I went up to the nurses' station to ask whether a package had arrived, I could not help but notice that they were enjoying my magazines and cookies and coffee cake. One of them was even reading one of my books!"

"I understand this has been difficult for you, these past few months. Losing the entirety of family is never something one ought to go through, and the psychological impacts of such can wreak havoc on our minds in ways that we cannot fully understand."

Shirley stared at him, trying to comprehend what he was saying. He took a sip of water and brushed off a drop that fell onto his festive, knitted vest.

"You're a bright girl. I assume you have taken basic psychology classes as part of your curriculum at the University of Pennsylvania. Tell me, have you heard of the study done on mice whereby, after being moved from a familiar to an unfamiliar environment, the mice no longer recognize their food, even when the same food granules they have always eaten are presented in the same dishes they have always used?"

She shook her head no.

"Well, the findings of the study suggested that changing the environment that the mice were accustomed to inhibited their ability to recognize what they were familiar with, meaning that the stress of the shift impacted their judgment. In other words, they could not see the forest for the trees. In many ways, you have experienced what the mice have. You have had a very large and sudden alteration in your life, and it is very possible, in my opinion, that you experienced a consequential shift in your perception of events around you. Do you see what I am saying?"

She thought for a moment. It did make sense. She had viewed life differently after the accident and often felt aloof from the world around her. But still, what were the chances of such a coincidence with the package?

"Those were my things," she insisted.

"I must tell you that I visited the nurses' station right after this transpired, listening to the nurses' side of the story. The only food I noticed was some leftover dinner from the kitchen, which they are always offered. I believe they had potatoes and beef, if I am not mistaken. I observed neither cookies nor cake and have no recollection of magazines or books…only patient charts, which they were busily completing before their shift change.”

“I can promise you I am not making up what I saw,” Shirley said defensively.

“No one believes you made it up. But perhaps you just think you saw something that you really did not. Perhaps your stress cloaked what was really before you, leading you to see something different…similar to the mice in the study.”

“What would that mean if that is the case…if I’m seeing what’s not there? Am I schizophrenic?” She knew the term well, and a sudden fear sent shivers running down her spine as she wondered whether her paranoia and hallucinations pointed to something more sinister than stress. Her mother’s sister, Catherine, had suffered for decades from the mental illness and spent most of her adulthood institutionalized, never well enough to leave before her death.

The question seemed to surprise Dr. Richter. “No, of course not. Such a diagnosis takes time to adequately diagnose. What happened last night could very well just be an outward presentation of grief and an uncertainty over how to progress in a world you no longer recognize.”

“Well, if the nurses didn’t take my package, where could it be?”

“Actually, I believe the postal service did deliver something for you, earlier this morning.” Dr. Richter got up and pushed a speaker button on the wall. “Mary, bring in Ms. Fitzpatrick’s items, would you?” He returned to his seat, and a moment later, a woman in white garb emerged with a box, dropping it next to the doctor before shutting the door behind her. “I had the nurses open it, as we do for all packages, just to make sure there is nothing dangerous inside, but I think this should rest your mind considerably.”

Shirley pulled the package by the lip over to her chair. She pulled out two boxes of chocolates, some candy canes, snickerdoodles, a couple of *Good Housekeeping* magazines, and three romance novels, which included *It's A Great World* by Emilie Loring, which she had been dying to read.

"Is that what you were expecting?"

"Why, yes," Shirley responded, excited to receive the package but undeniably mortified. "I'm so sorry for my behavior and for making an absolute fool of myself."

"We have all seen it before, and it is nothing we cannot handle," he said with a smile. "Before you go, how are you tolerating your medications? Are you experiencing any side effects, like dizziness, nausea, hallucinations…that sort of thing?"

She thought of the snakes, those retched things, that were plaguing her much of the time now, but a gut feeling told her to keep quiet, at least for the moment.

"No, I'm doing just fine."

She noticed a look on his face as he jotted down a few notes, almost as if he had expected her to have *some* symptoms, and was surprised that she did not.

Shirley returned to her room right after the visit with Dr. Richter. Barbara was off in one of her sessions, so she had the room to herself for a few hours. She reread the card that the sorority had sent, thankful that she had friends who cared enough to send her gifts, despite her mental breakdown. "We wish you all the best and think of you every day. We cannot wait to see you when you are well. Enjoy the magazines, books, and desserts! Merry Christmas!"

As she held the box, she noticed something peculiar. Her name and address were nowhere to be found. The cardboard was blank, lacking even a shipping label. So how had it been delivered? Surely, there was some explanation for it, and she decided it best to let it go.

Shirley slipped under the sheets for an afternoon nap. She had gotten into the habit of covering her head while she slept. For a moment, in the darkness, she could pretend to be home, in a life that was normal. Sometimes, she could even fool herself into believing that she was at her parents' house, just waking up to the smell of eggs and pancakes cooking downstairs. And while lost in the make-believe world that hid beneath her sheets, there were no snakes. It was as if those hideous creatures ceased to exist, perhaps aware that it was off limits.

It was Christmas morning. Cynthia emerged just after six for morning medications. She said very little, handing Barbara and Shirley their pills one at a time, observing them closely as they swallowed. Neither had slept well. After dinner, both had fallen asleep, only to wake several times during the night. Barbara rubbed her eyes as she downed the white and gray pills, the two brown tablets, the shiny green capsule, and the pink pill.

Shirley yawned as she consumed the same. "What about the blue one?" she asked, noticing that it was missing.

"Dr. Richter asked for it to be discontinued," Cynthia replied bluntly, surprisingly bothering to answer the question.

"Are there children here?" Barbara asked. "Shirley and I both thought we heard children all night in the attic. They were so loud, running about up there. We barely slept."

For a second, the corners of Cynthia's mouth turn up in a slight smile, as though she found pleasure in the prospect of children running about at all hours of the night, keeping other patients awake. And then, just as quickly, before Shirley could be sure of what she was witnessing, her face returned to its usual frown.

"There are no children here," she replied gruffly. Too many questions were being asked. Her job was to provide medications and see to it that the women did as they were told while hospitalized, not to engage in trivial conversation.

"But we heard them," Barbara insisted.

"Old pipes, perhaps, but not children, *that* I can assure you." Upon reaching the door, Cynthia realized she had left her pill tray on Shirley's bed and begrudgingly stomped her way over and back again, her nurse's uniform far too tight at the seams and threatening to sever at any moment, before closing the door behind her. Barbara and Shirley looked at each other and a simultaneous giggle erupted from their mouths. What a strange woman Cynthia was.

"Do you think she acts this way around her family?" Shirley asked.

"I doubt she has a family. She probably lives alone with her cats."

The two women shared a laugh. Shirley normally would not have made fun of someone, but a little joy at someone else's expense seemed allowable given their current situation.

"I wonder what happened in her life to make her so bitter."

"An old harridan, that's what she is," Barbara added. "Goodness, I hope I don't ever become that intolerable."

Most patients spent the holiday visiting with family, and the first floor was bustling with people coming and going, wearing their Sunday best. Patients who had no visitors were given the option of working in Francis Hall, which Barbara and Shirley both gladly accepted rather than remain secluded in their rooms. A few other family-less souls worked busily away in the loft while the two women baked rolls. It was a day they had all dreaded, and keeping busy made it pass more quickly.

"So, if you don't mind my asking, where's your family?" Shirley asked, her hands busy kneading the dough of the next batch. She did not know much about Barbara's home situation other than no one was coming to see her for the holidays either. But there was an immediate sense of regret as soon as the words left her mouth. Barbara's face dropped. She had known her for less than a week and should have known better than to bring up something so personal this soon.

"They want nothing to do with me. I guess you could say I'm the black sheep of the family."

Shirley wondered how anyone could not want to be around this woman. She was kind and had a wonderful sense of humor. On top of that, she was a talented musician.

"Goodness, I'm sorry! But it can't be as bad as all that." The idea that she was disliked by anyone seemed preposterous.

"But it's true. I've been disowned." Despite the freezing weather outside, it was hot in the kitchen. Sweat beaded along her forehead, and she wiped a handkerchief across her face. It was obvious that Barbara needed someone to talk to, someone to listen.

"Here, sit down. The rolls can wait." The two women sat at a small table, and for a few minutes, neither said anything.

Barbara lit up a cigarette, which shook nervously in her hand. "I'm sorry."

"There's no need to apologize. I'm here if you want to talk."

"My family wanted nothing to do with me after my last divorce. But if they only knew the truth. I deserve it. I'm so ashamed."

"It can't be as bad as all that," Shirley comforted, taking her hand in her own.

"I killed my baby," she whispered, so quietly that at first, Shirley thought she had misheard. A cry of unbearable pain followed, and a nurse came running from the loft to find out what had happened. Barbara quickly shooed him away, insisting she had simply dropped a rolling pin on her foot, which was a good enough explanation for someone forced to work on Christmas. "I'm sorry I'm bombarding you with this," she huffed.

Shirley struggled to comprehend what Barbara was telling her. "What do you mean, you killed your baby?"

"I didn't want to do it. I begged Jerome, my ex-husband, to let me keep it, but he wouldn't hear of it. He didn't want a child in our lives. And to be honest, when we got married, neither did I. I thought that we were enough for each other and that there was no need for anyone else besides the two of us. But when I found out I was pregnant, it all changed. I suddenly wanted to be a mother in the worst way, and I wanted for him to *want* to be a dad, but he didn't want any part of it. He told me that if I didn't get rid of it, he'd leave me." She laughed. "He left me anyways. He drove me to a doctor who ran operations out of his basement and listened to music in the car while I...let them take our child," she cried. "I kept telling myself it was for the marriage, that if I did what he wanted, our problems would go away, but the truth of it is that a piece of me died that day, too, and I hated him for it. Afterwards, I couldn't stand to even be in the same damn room as him. When I looked at him, I felt sick. Would our baby have had his eyes? His smile?"

Shirley held Barbara close. "I'm terribly sorry you went through that."

"I believe he regretted it, too. We constantly fought afterwards about the smallest things. A few weeks later, he went to the store for cigarettes and never came back. The next time I saw him was at the courthouse, finalizing our divorce. My parents were not supportive and blamed me for it. *A twice-divorced daughter? Once is bad enough. What will people think of us?* Afterwards, they completely shut me out. I coped the best I could. I took sleeping pills and slept months of my life away, hoping to not wake up. I smoked. I drank. One night, I woke up in a gutter and had no idea how I got there, and I didn't even care what had happened to me. All I could think about was my baby, who should have been born that month." She tapped a long bit of ash off the cigarette, inhaled a deep drag, and then, quite matter-of-factly, continued, "And then, one morning, I woke up around six thirty and walked a mile to a busy bridge. I watched the river below, thinking how easy it would be to jump and have all of my problems vanish in an instant. I felt there was nothing left for me in this life. But just as I was about to let go, a young fellow, who happened to be driving by on his way to work, got out and pulled me from the edge. So here I am. Now I'm their *crazy*, divorced daughter," she said with a subtle laugh, "and an utter embarrassment to the family."

"That seems particularly harsh if you want my opinion. I can't imagine." And she truly could not imagine her own parents caring more about their reputation than her wellbeing.

"Well, it is what it is. Some days, I feel I deserve it. I abandoned my child, and they abandoned me." Both sat quietly as Barbara dabbed her eyes and sniffled. "Thank you for listening. If you don't mind my asking, where's your family?"

"They died." The words still sounded unreal, like a story that was not her own. "My parents were on the American Airlines flight that crashed in October."

"I heard about that. It was all over the news. How terrible."

"Yeah. I still can't believe they're gone."

"Do you have any other family?"

"Nope, it was just the three of us, and now it's only me. My mom had a sister, but she died some years back." Shirley decided it best to leave out the part about her aunt's debilitating schizophrenia for now.

"How are you coping?" Barbara snuffed out the last of her cigarette.

"It's tough. Some days are good, others not so much." She held up her scarred wrists. And if she was honest with herself, the bad days lately had far outnumbered the good. She had no one, not even Sean, and a pang of guilt over having let an engagement slip away was starting to eat at her. Not that she missed their soured relationship. It was more of a realization that their breakup came with the hefty price of not having the support that she needed so desperately. And a certain resentment was growing over the fact that the career she had given it all up for was suddenly slipping away. For the first time, she questioned her drive for success outside of the home.

The women continued to chat over fresh dough and poppy seeds, completing the final batch of rolls just before three o'clock. They still had two hours left before they were expected back in the main hospital.

The voice of a young male nurse came from across the room. "Ladies, you are welcome to join us if you'd like." A large wooden table, typically used for boxing items prior to shipment, sat in the adjacent room. Several other patients from the loft had already gathered around it. "Bring a basket of those sweet rolls with you."

Shirley could see that the table was adorned with a spruce runner, red roses, a turkey, potatoes, bean casserole, stuffing, pastries, and eggnog.

"Where did all this come from?" Shirley asked, amazed to see so much warm food that had obviously not come from the kitchen.

"It's a gift," the nurse answered. He lit a cigarette and offered the women one, and Barbara accepted. He was only slightly older and had the shoulders of a linebacker. His blonde hair was parted to the side, his face clean shaven. There was a genuine kindness in his eyes, a stark contrast to Cynthia and the other nurses at Chastain Park.

"Robert did this last year, too. Had Christmas dinner delivered for those of us without families," an older woman from the table called out. Her torso moved back and forth uncontrollably, and her hand shook as she reached for a plate.

"Let me help you, Judy," Robert offered, gathering a plate and filling it with a little bit of each food.

"This is very generous of you," Shirley responded. "Why have I not seen you before?"

"I'm typically relegated to the men's unit. I've also been away for the past two weeks caring for my sick mother."

"Oh, I'm sorry. This is wonderful. Thank you."

Barbara and Shirley carried over a batch of rolls, and a young man of about twenty helped himself to two. A middle-aged man with no teeth sat beside him and dunked his food in his water glass between bites, taking a swig of his cigarette from time to time. A similarly-aged woman sat at the end of the table, staring off into space, as if sleeping with her eyes open. It was only when she smiled that Shirley could tell she was listening to those around her.

The young man with two rolls seemed like any other student she would encounter back at school, smart enough and confident. She wondered why he was institutionalized. It would not be until weeks later that she would hear about his story through the grapevine. Johnny MacIntyre had been born with epilepsy and given up by his parents when they learned of his diagnosis, afraid they could not properly care for him. He had grown up moving from one institution to the next, deemed a warden of the state due to his condition. Looking back at that Christmas dinner, Shirley would find herself amazed by how well he thrived, despite his diagnosis, with a healthy disdain for the system that kept him imprisoned because of it. She would catch herself imagining what he could have achieved if his parents had chosen to raise him along with their other children instead of washing their hands of what they saw as a difficulty. Would he have been a doctor or a lawyer, maybe? Or perhaps a mathematician? The world would never know while he sat like a butterfly in a cage.

Shirley would learn through the same grapevine that Judy Robinson had been left by her family when they discovered she had cerebral palsy four days after birth. She had never known the outside world. Chastain Park was the only home…the only family…she had ever had. Yet she showed no contempt at the cards she had been delt. She had lived a confined but happy life and knew no different anyways.

Walter Cummings, the man with the toothless grin, had lost his wife and two children in a house fire decades before and had suffered from debilitating depression ever since. He led a productive life in the institution, prompting his release several times over the years, only to be readmitted following suicide attempts. His only chance at a semi-normal life was within the confines of the asylum walls.

And Dorothy Johnson, the woman who looked at everything but nothing, had endured abuse at the hands of a husband with a short temper and an alcohol addiction. One night, as she put her boys to bed, he had come into the room, swinging a bottle of liquor around as he drunkenly sang a tune, waking up the children. According to what the children had told police, she had complained that he was keeping them awake and begged him to be quiet. Her husband reportedly grew irate. No woman would tell him what to do. He yelled and cussed as Dorothy tucked the boys in for a second time, and his yelling continued down the hallway to the den. The boys heard their mother, for the first time, yell back. Then came the loud thump against the wall and the screams. One of the boys was able to sneak into the kitchen and call the police, and when they arrived, they found Dorothy nearly dead, having been beaten mercilessly with the liquor bottle. Her head sat in a puddle of blood, and when she tried to speak, blood gurgled up and over her lips. It was the worst case of domestic violence the police had ever seen.

Dorothy survived, but not without suffering a severe brain injury that left her dependent on twenty-four-hour care. Her boys went to live with her mother, while her husband was incarcerated. At first, they came to see her twice a month, but she did not remember anything about her life or even her own boys' names, and over time, their visits became less frequent. They were now grown with their own families, and it was easier for them to just move on and forget.

It was rare for anyone new to join the group of four, who had come together to celebrate Christmas together in the barn for years now. They had taken Robert under their wings two years prior, and in many ways, they had become his family. Shortly after his father died, his mother had been diagnosed with breast cancer and given six months to a year to live. She had grown bitter from her sudden misfortunes, feeling as though God had forsaken her, and often took out her angst on her son as her health declined. Robert had not realized how much *he* needed the group, to have a holiday without the threat of death around the corner.

Over the next two hours, Robert and the forgotten ones celebrated together as a family. There was laughter and dancing around an impromptu faux Christmas tree and an old radio that played Christmas music. No one thought about loneliness or despair, broken families, damaged relationships, or debilitating illness. They were home, and all was right with the world.

Chapter Eight

A series of knocks came from the door of Dr. Richter's office. He ignored them, lying down on the loveseat, hoping that whoever stood on the outside had not seen him enter and would leave. A moment or two of undisturbed peace was all he needed. The knocking came once more before stopping entirely, the undetermined knocker apparently having given up.

The last few days had been an exhausting endeavor of tolerating the incessant bickering of his mother, who always managed to find inadequacies in Mariam's generosity and housekeeping. One day, the linens were not being changed often enough. The next, the meatloaf and coleslaw were intolerable. Then, Mariam had not removed the stain from her favorite white blouse. And on Christmas morning, the gifts were a disappointment. Mariam was growing tired of it, too. When he had left the house that morning, he felt a sense of guilt leaving her behind in what had become a toxic environment of his own creation.

The morning prior, Ruth had pulled apart the paper from her first gift with careless rigor, eager to indulge in the lucrativeness of Christmas. A scarf, its white, black, and red strands beautifully knitted into a plaid design, had been purchased months prior from a little shop in town. Mariam had thought that the colors and style of it complimented Ruth's wardrobe perfectly. But without giving it more than two seconds of judgment, she thanklessly cast it aside, stating that she already owned a similar piece and would have to exchange it. As per usual these days, Mariam was quick to apologize and offered to go into town the following day to return it.

Surely, the second gift would be exactly what Ruth wanted. The ruby and sapphire ring was an artistic piece of Mariam's making. She had taken the time to work with a local jeweler, even using an imported ruby with a unique history as the center stone. There was nothing to dislike about it, as far as she was concerned. She and Carl watched nervously as Ruth tore off the white and gold wrapping.

"Those stones on the sides are sapphires. And the ruby came from an auction." Mariam proudly explained.

"An auction?" she asked, seeming unamused. "You mean it's used?"

"No. Well, yes," Mariam continued, growing flustered. "Do you want to tell her?" she asked Carl. It was the first royal auction either had ever participated in, and it had cost them a pretty penny to come out as the winners. They had outbid seventeen other bidders and spent almost a thousand dollars for it, much more than they had planned or could afford at the moment, but it was to be a combined Christmas and eightieth birthday present, and they wanted to make it special.

"Very rarely, jewels are sold on behalf of the Bavarian royal family. When we traveled to Europe last summer, we attended an auction in Germany and purchased this ruby, which once belonged to Queen Therese of Bavaria, who reigned in the late nineteenth century. We were told it came from one of the rubies in her crown." The enthusiasm in his voice indicated just how proud he was of the gift. When he and Mariam had purchased it, they were certain Ruth would love it. She had been enamored with various royal families for as long as he could remember and thoroughly enjoyed any book or magazine pertaining to royalty.

"It's lovely," she said flatly, holding the ring up and examining it in the light. It was a dark ruby cut into the shape of an emerald. It was unlike any jewelry she had ever owned, so what she said next shocked everyone. "But I don't particularly care for rubies. Perhaps you can have it changed out for a blue sapphire. I'm fond of those, you know."

Carl and Mariam's jaws dropped.

"Mother, it belonged to Bavarian royalty," Carl repeated, in case she had missed that key piece of information. "You love royal families."

Ruth hardly seemed to notice the visible dismay on the faces before her. "Your dad, he always got me the nicest things. It's too bad he's not here with us." One minute, he was a saint, and the next, he never cared for anyone but himself, but today, he was apparently the former. "Do you remember that necklace he bought me for our last anniversary…the one with the emeralds? He always knew what I liked."

Mariam was growing exasperated with Ruth. "Would you like for me to bring it back to the jeweler then and have it redone?" she asked, struggling to hide her annoyance in her tone.

"Yes, if it's not too much to ask," she said sweetly. She gave Carl a smile, and Mariam half expected her to pinch his cheek while she was at it. The nerve of that woman. Ruth's rudeness was unbearable, and she excused herself to the kitchen. The boys would be over in an hour, and she had cinnamon rolls to bake and eggs and bacon to cook.

"Mariam is so sensitive," Ruth whispered to Carl.

He was a smart man and could see how his mother manipulated his wife, but the second he stood up to her, he knew she would assume the role of victim and make him feel like a horrible son. So, he said nothing, but sometimes, even silence has consequences. That night, Mariam did not speak to him, and as he lied in his office the next morning, he felt angry. All the things he could not say, all the guilt trips, a lifetime of having to tiptoe around a narcissistic mother who, despite her best efforts to feign love, really did not love him at all. He hated her for it but knew that when he went home later that evening, he would put a smile on his face and act as if everything was normal.

The knocking on the door started up again, more urgently. He ignored it at first, but the knocker this time was more insistent.

"Come in, for God's sake!" he finally yelled, sitting up, and the door flung open. It was Cynthia.

"Why didn't you answer, doctor?"

"I'm busy. What is it?"

She closed the door behind her and sat down, irritated that she had been left waiting. She had thought about leaving, but it could not wait.

"There is something we need to talk about."

"What is it?" he asked, his frustration at having been interrupted visible. His mood swings lately had left her unsure whether she would be met with pleasantries or anger, and despite her outward toughness, the volatility of his behavior was starting to grate on her.

"It has to do with one of the male nurses…Robert, from Townsend Hall."

Dr. Richter looked up for the first time since Cynthia entered, lowering his glasses.

"Robert Patterson? Yes, a fine young man. He's done great work with the men's epileptic group, hasn't he?"

"Why yes, but it has come to my attention that he has grown close to several of our patients. Walter Cummings was overheard last night talking about a private Christmas dinner that was apparently shared by Robert and a group of patients out in the barn. We simply cannot allow a mingling of that sort to take place."

"Interesting. I was not made aware of this gathering. Which patients partook in this affair?"

"After questioning Mr. Cummings, I learned that there were six of them, in addition to Robert. Johnny MacIntyre, Judy Robinson,

Walter Cummings, Dorothy Johnson, Barbara Walker, and Shirley Fitzpatrick."

"Well, Dorothy Johnson does not possess the mental capacity to decipher right from wrong, so we mustn't blame her for any misconduct," he mused.

"You do see the problem here, doctor?" Cynthia's face grew sterner, her eyes looking as though they might jump out and attack Dr. Richter if he did not come to a quick realization of what she was saying.

"Yes, of course," he said in earnest, attempting to squash any question as to whether he grasped the possible implications of such a relationship.

Cynthia nodded in agreement. "I'm glad you understand. That is why I have decided, with your permission, to send each of the patients to solitary confinement for the course of one evening so that adventures of this sort are avoided in the future."

"I concur with your sentiment. Doing so will send a clear message to others that such behavior will not be tolerated. With the exception of Dorothy, and Judy given her physical limitations, you may arrange for a night of isolation as punishment. And as for Mr. Patterson, I would like to speak with him at once. Please send him up."

"Yes, doctor."

Cynthia stood up, adjusting her dress before exiting. It was impeccably starched and stainless, like the dressings of an angel, quite the contrast to the cold, hardened face that popped from the top.

Barbara and Shirley sat down for breakfast beside Regina, who greeted them with a smile. She had dark circles under her eyes, and they wondered whether she had been having problems sleeping.

They had not seen her over the holidays and had given her absence little consideration, assuming that she had been busy receiving visitors.

Minutes earlier, the duo had downed their identical morning pills, unceremoniously delivered by Cynthia, who was in a particularly sour mood and had not so much as said a single word upon entering. Both had taken the white and gray pills and two brown tablets, followed by the shiny green capsule and spotted pink pill. They no longer questioned what they were receiving for fear of her scorn. It was easier to just do as they were told and remain silent.

"How was your Christmas?" Barbara asked Regina. She was curious whether her sister had stopped by…or perhaps, she had met her mother's new boyfriend, the one who rode motorcycles and had arms covered in tattoos, the consequence of her mother's midlife crisis. But Regina seemed not to notice the question. Her mind was relegated to something else in the room of far greater interest.

"Aren't they just the sweetest?" she responded, sounding much calmer than the last time they spoke.

"Who?" Barbara asked, bewildered.

She followed Regina's gaze to the table where the witches sat. Thelma and Pearl had both braided their brown hair into similar styles and, from a distance, appeared eerily similar. June wore a new, bright red lipstick, perhaps given to her by someone special as a gift. Regina smiled and waved unabashedly in their direction. Thelma slowly lifted her hand in a half wave and resumed eating her buttered toast and eggs, looking over every few seconds at Regina, who joyfully continued to watch the group.

"Stop it," Barbara demanded, wondering whether her friend was trying to get them all hexed. "They're looking our way."

Regina continued to look fondly upon the witches, her smile unwavering, throwing another awkward wave in from time to time whenever one of the women looked up. Her behavior was making the trio just as nervous as it was making Barbara and Shirley.

"For goodness's sake, what's wrong with you?" Shirley asked. She and Barbara looked at each other, confused by her sudden infatuation with the women whom she was too afraid to look at only days before.

"What have they done to you?" Barbara asked seriously.

"Why, you are a comedian," Regina laughed, seemingly amused that something so ridiculous had been suggested. "They're actually quite friendly, if you'd just give them a chance."

"I don't understand," Shirley continued. Then, in a lowered voice, "You don't like them, and they don't like you, remember?"

Regina turned to face her. "Why, how silly. We get along splendidly."

Barbara and Shirley looked at each other, confused. Was she experiencing some sort of break with reality? Or had the witches, in fact, managed to cast a spell on her? At this point, both seemed equally possible, the latter far more frightening than the first.

"Did Shirley tell you about how the nurses took her package?" Barbara asked, changing the subject.

"Well, I ended up getting it after all. It seems it was all just some big misunderstanding." The situation had become a source of embarrassment for Shirley, to the point that she had decided to keep the entire incident to herself going forward unless pressed to discuss it.

"So, they didn't take it?" Barbara confirmed.

"No, but something was off about it all. I just can't put my finger on it."

Regina waved at another group of women beside them, giving them her best smile, and then turned to the nursing staff who stood beside the door, giving them their own dose of excessive friendliness. The nurses looked in her direction but showed no other signs of acknowledgment other than whispers exchanged amongst each other, in all obviousness regarding her. Shirley wondered what they were saying and would have paid a pretty penny to hear a tidbit of their conversation.

"Did your family come by over Christmas?" Barbara asked, once again, eager to break the awkwardness of the conversation and to find out where she had been the past two days.

"Family?" Regina smiled sweetly at the two, her missing front tooth more noticeable than ever. "Why, no. My sister decided to spend the holiday with her husband's family, and my brother is skiing in the Swiss Alps…or is it the French Alps? Who knows, really? Mom and Joey made their excuses. Anyways, it's probably for the best. I had a little procedure done and haven't felt up for guests."

"Procedure? What do you mean, if you don't mind my asking?" Shirley was almost afraid to ask, but genuine curiosity regarding Regina's strange behavior broke any barriers, and the question flowed out before she could stop it.

"I can't remember what they called it, but they told me it was to help control my moods," she laughed. "They inserted a tool through my eye and into my brain. Anyway, I feel much better now. Dr. Richter says I may even be able to go home soon, once the bruising gets better."

Shirley shuttered to think about the procedure Regina described. She knew it all too well. A lobotomy had been performed on her aunt, leaving her a shell of her former self in her final years. The once-vibrant woman everyone loved, despite her odd hallucinations, slipped away into an agreeable vegetable with the personality of a drumstick. And while the new and improved Regina appeared alive and well, Shirley understood that the real Regina was gone.

The trio said nothing for the remainder of the meal. Shirley picked at her eggs and bacon, no longer hungry. Barbara did not eat much more than her. Regina continued to smile and wave to those around her in ignorant bliss until they were shoved off to their respective therapy sessions for the day.

Barbara and Shirley were each separately reprimanded during their sessions with Dr. Richter for participating in the barn Christmas party. It was unthinkable, absolutely absurd, that patients and staff would intermingle. It was dangerous, they were told.

"You are here for recovery, not social visits," he scolded sternly, to which Barbara rolled her eyes and Shirley apologized. He took great care to note their different reactions to the admonishment and jotted his observation, along with the date and time, down in his notebook. He kept his promise to Cynthia and punished each patient who participated in the celebration, except for the physically and mentally disabled Judy Robinson and Dorothy Johnson, with a night of solitary confinement.

Directly after dinner, Cynthia knocked on the bedroom door and, with a gleeful strut, led them away for their punishment, down the hallway and into the stairwell, this time up the stairs, rather than down. Neither had been past the second floor as the third, the attic, was strictly off limits.

The heavy stairwell door creaked open, sounding as though it had not been opened in a half century, and Cynthia flipped on the solitary bulbs, which hung ungraciously from the rafters, revealing a neglected level long left to bugs and rodents. Exposed framing and uncovered insulation occupied the space above their heads as they walked down a narrow corridor with a row of small quarters off to the right, separated only by boards of plywood and resembling something closer to horse stalls than patient rooms. The floors were a simple subfloor, barren of carpets or rugs, filled with years of dust and the droppings of vermin. Cobwebs occupied the corners and hung in droopy canopies, nearly snatching Cynthia's nurse cap right off her head as she walked by.

"You are to take this room," Cynthia instructed, grabbing Shirley's arm and pushing her into the first of the isolation chambers. She locked a simple, plywood door behind her. "And you," she grabbed Barbara's arm, "are to stay in this one," she said, pushing her into the adjacent room. She instructed the women that they were to spend their evening contemplating their behavior on Christmas and were forbidden from talking amongst each other. They would be checked on periodically, and if any noises were heard, they risked extending their confinement further. Lastly, she informed them that should they have to use the restroom, they were to ring the bell that hung from the rafters between their rooms.

"But how do I reach it?" Shirley asked, puzzled as to how she could possibly reach up that high.

"You'll just have to move the bed," Cynthia instructed, referring to a small cot that sat on the other side of the room. "There used to be a rope, but…," she paused briefly, "you can probably muster why that was removed."

The women were silent. Had someone hung themselves here? How would they ever be able to sleep where something like that happened? Suddenly, the lights flipped off, and the door to the stairwell slammed shut behind Cynthia. The entire attic was cast into pitch-black darkness. The windows on either end of the attic were useless as it had already been dark outside for hours. Even the stars hid in obscurity behind the overcast sky.

"What do we do now?" Shirley asked in a whisper.

"Oh, I don't know. Think about the person that hung themselves where we are sleeping," Barbara answered sarcastically. "How are we supposed to sleep here now?"

"I don't think we're supposed to. We're being punished, remember?"

"Do you think the others are coming up here, too?"

"I don't know," Shirley answered. "Is there anyone else up here?" she called around the attic. A shiver ran down her spine as she recalled hearing children playing in the attic the other night.

"Shhh," Barbara scolded. "They'll hear you down there."

There was no answer. It was silent, a little too silent. They could hear nothing of the hustle and bustle taking place below. Surely, it was almost time for the nurses to clock out for the evening, and they were likely finishing their notes over snacks and chatter right about now. But they could hear none of it. Just the occasional howl of the wind from the window fifteen feet away.

Barbara felt her way over to the cot. It creaked when she sat and every time she moved. Shirley lingered by the shared wall a moment longer. Even though she could not see Barbara, it felt good to be close to someone.

"It's cold up here, isn't it?" she asked, back to a whisper. She rubbed her arms, trying to warm up.

"Yes, at least the cot has some blankets." Barbara had wrapped her body in the comforter. Her nose was cold, but her body had quickly warmed up.

Shirley fumbled her way to her own cot and, taking Barbara's advice, wrapped herself in the comforter. It was warm as promised but had a stale smell, as if it had not been washed for some time. She made her way back to the wall and sat bundled on the floor.

"I think it's just ridiculous that they put us in isolation for celebrating Christmas. Absolute nonsense, if you ask me." Barbara stuck out her bottom lip and huffed a clump of hair out of her face. Oh, what she would have done for a smoke right now, but she had left her cigarettes in the room. It was going to make for a very long evening.

"Yeah, hard to believe." Shirley wondered what her parents would have thought about what was happening to her. Perhaps they knew. She had felt their presence around her lately, more strongly at certain times than others, and she wondered whether it was the two of them she sensed in the attic with her just then.

"Hey, why don't you sing for me," Shirley asked, changing the subject and somewhat embarrassed that she had not asked before now, given that Barbara was a talented musician.

"I don't have my guitar, obviously, but as long as you don't mind, it might help us pass the time."

"No, of course not." It had been ages since she had heard live music and likely longer since the hospital had, if ever.

"I wrote this back when Jerome and I were going through our divorce. It's called *Fooled*. She cleared her throat. There was silence for a moment, and then, quietly, that first pitch in a country twang that Shirley imagined complimented the guitar just fine.

Hey there, honey
Where you been
Can't stop thinkin'
Of my best friend

I looked for you
Where did you go
Need you more than ever
But I don't know

Please don't go-o
Please don't go

Took my life
And took my soul
Without you, honey
I've grown cold

Made me forget
Wrong from right
Now I'm staying
Up all night

Please don't go-o
Please don't go

Everything's changed
Nothing's the same
What you took
Made me go insane

Go on and leave
Please don't come back
You're lost to me
There's no healing that

Please don't go-o
Please don't go

What rotten luck
I saw her at the store

Big bellied, on your arm
Just walk out that door

Just go-o
Just go

When the song was finished, Shirley had tears in her eyes that she dabbed dry with an edge of the comforter. "That was beautiful…and so sad. Is it true?"

Barbara was quiet. She had sung the song so many times that the stabbing pain that once came with uttering the lyrics had faded, at least enough that she could get through the song like any other. It had become a hit at the Blue Bird. She suspected that many of the women in her audience had similar stories that they kept hidden, and this was the closest they got to finding comradery in their suffering.

"Thank you, thank you," she said modestly, feigning a bow. "Yeah, every bit of it."

"Are you okay?"

"I don't know if I'll ever be, honestly."

The women talked briefly about Regina and her new therapy and were soon off to sleep, far earlier than usual, but with nothing to do and the lights out, there was no reason to stay up. Neither knew exactly what time it was when they were awakened by the noises.

It was still so very dark. A shimmer of moonlight escaped the clouds and provided just enough light to make out their surroundings. Shirley's hands were ice cold, and Barbara's feet, which extended far past the end of the comforter, had begun to numb.

"Did you hear that?" Shirley whispered, hoping Barbara was awake.

"What was that?" Barbara had heard it, too. Something or someone was moving around the attic.

"I don't know."

The women sat in silence, listening for any repetition of the sound. Suddenly, something shuffled past their doors. They held their breath, trying but not wanting to hear it. And then came the sound that could not be brushed off as the wind or stray critters…a little girl giggling.

"Who's there?" called Barbara. She looked around nervously. Though all was normal within the confines of her room, something lurked on the other side of the wall. A minute of silence passed, and just as the women began to think they had imagined it all, the sound of feet skipping along the corridor sent a shiver down their spines.

"Who's there?" Barbara repeated, her anxiety growing.

There would be no answer. But what followed did nothing to calm their fears. There were others. They ran this way and that, prancing around in darkness, hidden behind the stall walls. They talked to one another, too. The voice of a small child asked, "Can I play with the doll?"

"No," another meek voice answered. "Mine."

Both women were tense, silent, listening to the voices, so close yet invisible. It was not the first time they had heard them. In fact, they had heard them many times before, at night, during the darkest hours, and coming from the attic.

"Give me."

"No!" the voice presumably with the doll cried. "Mine!" it repeated.

Then came the voice of a boy who sounded a little older, maybe eight or nine. "Maddie, give it back. That's Caroline's. Take my teddy instead."

That seemed to resolve the conflict, at least for the moment, and the three quickly resumed their giggles and skipping, back and forth, and up and down, the attic corridor.

"Who are you?" Shirley asked, desperate to know who shared the attic with them, but once again, there was no answer. Her heart pounded, and an electricity in the air made the hair on her arms stand straight up. Barbara felt it, too.

Suddenly, Shirley had the feeling of falling, as if jumping from an airplane and hitting the ground with unmitigated impact. She screamed, only to find that she was still in the same spot on the attic floor. In a state of utter panic, she pushed her bed towards the wall and hit the bell hard with her fist. A loud, reverberating, church-bell chime rang throughout the attic, bouncing from one wall to the next. The unexpected decibel hit sent both women jumping, and yet, the children seemed to take no notice, continuing on with their play undeterred. Within thirty seconds, the heavy door of the stairwell swung open, creaking loudly and then banging forcefully against the wall with a loud thump. With the flip of a light switch, the voices and footsteps of the children abruptly ceased, as if they had never been there at all.

Cynthia unlocked Shirley's door first, demanding to know whether she had been the one to ring the bell.

"Who is up here with us?" Shirley asked, the stress of the event evident in her voice.

"No one else is up here besides you two," she answered gruffly. It was obvious she had been sleeping and was quite annoyed to have been awoken. It would have been a miracle if anyone in the hospital was still asleep. A long robe two sizes too small covered her body down to her feet, and her gray, wiry hair, always hidden under a nurse cap, hung down in an unfamiliar-looking, braided mess, making her nearly unrecognizable.

"We both heard it," Barbara objected from the other stall. "There were children, several of them, running about and fighting over toys. Two girls, Maddie and Caroline, and a boy."

"That's impossible." Cynthia paused for a moment, a look of intrigue upon her face. "There's no one else up here. Now, if that is all, go back to sleep," she commanded. How curious, she thought to herself, stifling the urge to ask for more details. She would tell Dr. Richter first thing in the morning, and if he saw fit, he would be the one to present questions.

"May I have a look?" Shirley asked, sticking her head out of the stall. Cynthia reluctantly allowed her to peer out the doorway into the rest of the attic. There was only emptiness. Plain old subfloor, wood framing, and insulation…no evidence of children or toys. Even the dust that had accumulated in a thin layer over the floor lacked any footprints besides their own. Shirley stared, baffled by the lack of evidence to support what they had heard.

Cynthia nudged her back into the stall before soundly relocking the door. The overhead lights went off, and once again, the attic returned to calm. A few minutes later, Barbara spoke.

"Are you still awake?"

"Yeah."

"I'm being punished for what I've done. I just know it."

"No, no, that's not it," Shirley answered. "I heard it, too, remember?"

It was nearly daybreak before they fell back asleep. There were no more voices that night, but neither could dismiss what they had heard. There had been children in the attic. Barbara and Shirley were sure of it. But who were they and where had they gone?

Just as soon as they closed their eyes came the muted sound of the intercom below, followed by the creaking of the stairwell door. The jingling of Cynthia's keys signaled the end of their solitary confinement. They had survived the night in the attic, but its mysteries left a sickening feeling in the pits of their stomachs.

Chapter Nine

The end of the Christmas holidays meant a return to routine at Chastain Park. There was a palpable sadness amongst the patients. Family visits and celebrations had come to an end, and many were faced with the harsh reality that it might be another year before they saw their loved ones again. Shirley was becoming more and more aware of just how isolating life at Chastain Park could be. Some patients would never leave the walls of the institution because of an inability or unwillingness of family to care for them, while others remained because they did not want to get better, perhaps out of fear of leaving the only place they had actually felt cared for.

The pill regimen was the same. That is, minus the shiny green capsule, which inexplicably disappeared from both Barbara and Shirley's orders. They swallowed the white and gray pills, two brown tablets, and sprinkled pink pill as requested and immediately were whisked off to breakfast, where there was a notable absence.

"Where's Regina?" Barbara asked.

"I don't know. I haven't seen her all morning. Maybe she has another procedure?"

The two women looked at each other, hoping that was not the case. How much more flaccid could she be? Her vacant disposition had scared them both. She was hollowed out, alive but not there, yet the medical team considered her progress a success. All done, problem solved, and yet, so broken.

As if in response, a dark sedan pulled up to the front of the hospital. Shirley and Barbara could see it from their table, which overlooked the vast landscape that separated the hospital from the rest of society. A young, red-headed woman emerged, wearing a gray dress suit, partially covered by a dark wool coat with a fur trim at the collar. She looked awfully out of place, much too fancy for the hospital. As she walked up the front steps, she stopped, as if making a last-minute decision about whether or not to proceed.

A loud voice greeted her at the door. It was Geraldine's. "Mrs. Rothbrook, how do you do?"

"Just fine, thank you. Please, call me Julia," she answered in a Southern accent.

Their voices grew harder to hear over the noise of the dining hall, yet Shirley and Barbara could see the women talking just outside the door in the lobby.

"You're sure she's better?" Julia seemed to ask.

Geraldine motioned Regina forward. She was hardly recognizable. She wore a green peacoat over slacks and carried a small suitcase. Her face bore makeup, hiding her freckles and the dark circles around her eyes, and her curly, red hair had been pulled back into an updo. The only familiar part of Regina was her missing tooth, the gap visible all the way from the table.

"How I've missed you," she seemed to say, hugging the woman named Julia. Next to each other, they looked nearly identical. There was no mistaking their relation.

"I can't thank you enough," Julia said, next embracing Geraldine before walking Regina out the door.

"Not even a goodbye," lamented Barbara as the car drove away.

"How peculiar," Shirley added.

There was another notable absence in the dining hall that morning. The witches' table sat empty amongst the crowded room, avoided by other diners like a contamination site. Everyone knew whose table it was, and no one dared take a seat.

"Dr. Richter," Cynthia began. Once again, she caught him first thing in the morning when he preferred to be alone in his office, able to work in undisturbed silence.

"What is it now?" he responded, irritated and hoping that her unannounced entries would not seek to become habit. It had been another rough night of dealing with some constant level of bickering between Mariam and his mother, and he just wanted a moment of peace and quiet.

"A bit sour this morning, are we?" She gazed at him from across the room for a moment before walking in his direction. "I have done as we discussed. Johnny MacIntyre and Walter Cummings were kept overnight in the basement holding stalls, and Barbara Walker and Shirley Fitzpatrick spent the night upstairs. Hopefully, that will act as a deterrent to any future sordid festivities."

At that, Dr. Richter looked up, suddenly intrigued by what Cynthia had to say. "You sent them to the *attic*? For heaven's sake, why?"

In case Dr. Richter had become upset by the news, she had prepared to remind him that the men and women were to be kept separated and that shared sleeping quarters was strictly prohibited per hospital protocol. She breathed a sigh of relief when she realized that he saw no fault in her decision and seemed, rather, to have a macabre appreciation for her choice of location.

"Those two women deserved to be set right." She smiled slyly. "I've had nothing but problems with them since they arrived, Shirley in particular. Were it not for that girl being here, I do believe Barbara would be far easier to handle."

"I take it they had a rough night of it," he chuckled. The two exchanged a glance, holding an unspoken conversation that no one else, were they present, would have been able to decipher. In his excitement, he kissed her on the cheek. The severity of her expression softened into a rare smile. She felt exhilarated, too, and the sick satisfaction of having done something so wrong. It was moments like this that fed their collective madness and nurtured an unsavory bond between them. They fed off each other in a way impossible with anyone else, the evil in their hearts rejuvenated each time.

"Yes, it seems so," she continued. "I was awoken at about three in the morning to the sound of one of the bells. You remember those bells between stalls?"

He nodded. How could he forget? It had been years since he had been to the attic, but he had spent enough time up there as a child that he remembered them perfectly. He had rung one of the patina-covered copper bells once and had been reprimanded so severely that he was afraid to even look at them as an adult.

"The women claimed to hear children outside of their stalls, running and playing about. Of course, there was no one. But they were insistent there were two girls, Maddie and Caroline, and a boy."

Dr. Richter's ears perked up. "A boy? How curious. Did they mention his name?"

"No, just that he was keeping them awake and playing with the two girls." She paused. "You don't think…" Suddenly, she felt silly for having even brought it up at all. It was preposterous. The very idea that those children were still there. It was a matter of impossibility. Even more humiliating was the fact that Dr. Richter had not stopped her…that he had allowed her to continue and embarrass herself in such a manner. "I'm sorry. I shouldn't have brought it up."

She quickly excused herself, closing the door quietly behind her, slipping away and out of sight for a moment to collect herself. Dr. Richter, meanwhile, stayed in his office with the door closed all morning. He canceled all of his appointments for the day and took a stroll along the hospital property after lunch. He had much to churn over in his mind, and this latest tidbit of information was enough to hijack his thoughts for the next week. But there was something else on his mind, too.

The weather had warmed to just above freezing, warmer in certain spots where the sun hit strongest, and the snow was rapidly melting, leaving the land a soupy mess of muddy slickness. He would ruin his work shoes, he knew it, and Mariam would scold him relentlessly for it. But given the stress of living with his mother…that bitch…and the toll it was taking on him, combined with the rather interesting tidbit from Cynthia, he needed to get out in the fresh air and be by himself for a while. He needed to think.

The night prior had been nearly as bad as Christmas. Earlier in the day, though it had pained her greatly, Mariam had dutifully taken the ruby ring to their local jeweler to have the ruby, the Bavarian royal family ruby, no less, replaced with an ordinary blue sapphire. Having no use for the ruby herself and hoping to offset the cost of the exchange, she had reluctantly sold it to the shop, handing over all of the papers of authenticity at the end of the transaction. The blue sapphire was exquisite, a fine gift indeed, and if she had purchased the sapphire ring to begin with, she would have been happy to gift it. But looking at it now, after all that Ruth had put her through, she hated it…despised it…and something deep inside of her snapped. For the first time in her life as a prim and proper woman, she lost it. In front of an unsuspecting couple exiting their car, she threw the ring hard against the asphalt. It clanked like a small bell. She picked it up and threw it again, finding it a moment later. The gold had small scratches and a dent that stood out in the sunlight like a glistening drop of dew.

The couple watched for a moment, not knowing what to make of the woman having a tantrum before them. She felt the cold sweat of a midlife hot flash and, without pause, placed the ring carefully behind the back tire of her car. The engine started up without hesitation, and the car began to move back and forth and back and forth over the ring, drawing the attention of a small crowd. A rather plump gentleman stood in the front and, in tour guide fashion, informed the others that she was driving over a ring. When she finally felt relief equivalent to slapping Ruth across the face, she stooped to gather up what remained of the ring.

"She picked it up," the gentleman said, informing the others of the obvious.

Mariam gave the crowd a smile and a cheerful wave and sat in her car for a moment, examining the twisted prongs and bent setting, before driving away.

"What was that all about?" an older gentleman asked his wife, who only shrugged.

"Women…they're all crazy, the whole lot of them," the plump gentleman offered. "That one belongs in the loony bin."

When Mariam arrived home that evening, she was unusually giddy, as if she had just won the lottery. Even Carl wondered what had gotten into her. For the first time in six months, she could breathe. The weight of a thousand pounds had been taken off of her shoulders. Her needs had been met…even if that required taking matters into her own hands.

When they sat down to dinner, Ruth was already complaining about how the stew smelled off and how the bread looked moldy. Her complaining had become quite routine, as had Mariam's anxiety as she worked like a frantic mouse on a wheel to please the unpleasable, but her smile remained, unwavering, like a permanent fixture on her face.

"I can assure you, Ruth, I just bought the food this morning. Eat up, won't you?"

Ruth gave her a strange look, but Mariam smiled in her direction anyhow.

"Oh, silly me, I forgot the drinks." Mariam giggled as she got up to grab the glasses of water from the counter.

"Carl, what's gotten into her?" Ruth whispered, casting Mariam a scowl. "She's cooky. She left me alone all afternoon, and now she's acting like a rambunctious unicorn. If you ask me, she's been seeing that single guy down the street." She waved a wrinkled, swollen finger in the general direction of the neighbor's house.

Despite her whispering, Mariam could hear every word, yet she continued to smile, for she had the most extravagant of surprises planned out for the evening. She set the water glasses down and then took a seat herself, spreading her napkin neatly over her lap. She shuffled around in her chair, getting comfortable for what promised to be an entertaining evening.

"Well, let's not keep the crickets waiting. Begin," she commanded of Ruth and Carl. The two began eating, Ruth a little hesitantly, looking up every so often to see whether Carl was observing the horrible struggle Mariam put her through, creating such unappetizing dishes for those she supposedly loved. She would never, in her day, have been caught dead serving such a disgusting stew. The meat had been hacked into large chunks, obviously minimal effort put into its preparation. The vegetables, which had been sauteed beforehand, were burnt, the peas nearly unrecognizable under a black shell. The carrots were far too large and had not even been peeled. And that bread. She held it up towards the chandelier, examining the greenish splotches that appeared in clusters. Mariam had sworn the food was new, but she knew better. After a few bites, she felt like she was going to be sick.

"Carl," she grabbed his wrist, looking as though the life had just been sucked right out of her, "do you see what she does to me?" She was no longer whispering. Mariam shot her an angry glance. "To you? And to think you've been working in that place all day, and this is what you have to come home to."

"Mother, stop it," Carl begged. He did not want to be caught in the middle of a feud between the two women. More often than not, he felt like a toy that two children fought over, one pulling his right arm and the other his left, stretching him to the breaking point while he suffered the damage.

"I will do no such thing," Ruth said angrily, her voice rising. It was high time she put her foot down. "The damned stew is burned. The bread is moldy. I wouldn't have given this to Toby." Toby was the German shepherd Carl had had growing up, the pet that was supposed to take the place of his brother when he…

"Ruth, you are being ridiculous," Mariam interjected in her own defense. There was no pleasing this woman. She experienced the world as she wanted, regardless of reality. "I bought the food this very morning, and I can assure you it's not burned…or moldy."

"Sure, it's fine," Ruth said, pushing her food away. "So is a needlepoint."

"What's that supposed to mean?" Mariam looked desperately at Carl, pleading with her eyes for him to step in, and it was not until she stomped hard on his foot that he engaged, though, "Mother, please," is all he mustered. He was tired of her relentless complaining, too, but, unlike Mariam, had developed a keen ability to tune her out.

Ruth reluctantly relented, returning to her stew as she sulked in silence. It was a few minutes before anyone spoke, and by that time, heart rates had dropped, and empty stomachs had begun to feel satiated. Mariam was not about to let Ruth's outbursts spoil her special surprise.

"Ruth, I had your ring fixed this afternoon." Mariam's smile returned as she handed over the same ring box that, just that morning, had held the precious Bavarian ruby.

"Oh, thank heavens for that." She grabbed the box ungratefully out of Mariam's hands and, for the first time that evening, smiled, her anticipation growing. The blue sapphire ring that she so desperately wanted was finally hers. The hoops *that* woman had made her jump through to get it, though, were ridiculous. If Mariam had bothered to listen, she would have gotten it right the first time. She would show it off at bridge tomorrow. The ring was sure to make the other women in the neighborhood ooh and ahh. She wanted everyone to remember that she was the mother of a successful physician who adored her above all else.

Carefully, Ruth lifted the lid. Her smile drooped, and her cheeks faded into a sickly paleness that even her blush could not hide. Her lips pursed but mumbled nothing. She struggled to comprehend what befell her eyes.

"What is it, mother? Don't you like it?" Carl asked, obliviously.

Ruth held up the ring, her hand trembling with anger, and glared angrily at Mariam. It was her fault. She had done this. He examined the dented gold and bent setting. What kind of ring had Mariam purchased? Was it some sort of joke? Or perhaps it was a new fashion.

"It is different, isn't it, Mariam?" He hoped it was simply a matter of poor fashion choice rather than some deliberate attempt to take a swipe at his mother.

"Different? It's hideous!" Ruth slammed the ring down on the table. "You did this on purpose. I told you exactly what I wanted, and you ruined it."

"Mother, you don't know that. Mariam would never…"

"How dare you question me, Carl George Richter. I am your mother, your own flesh and blood."

"I'm sorry, I didn't mean to imply…"

"Oh, if only your father could see this." Always better in death than in life, yet neither said anything when she brought up the husband she could not stand, afraid to upset her even more.

Mariam felt a sense of satisfaction that she had craved since Ruth moved in…vindication for the months of torment the old hag had put her through. And she was not about to spoil it by downplaying what she had done. She had stood up for herself for the first time, and she was going to savor this moment, even if it angered Carl.

"It's true. I did it," Mariam admitted. "And I'm not the least bit sorry."

"There, I was right, wasn't I?" Ruth responded, giving Carl a look that said, 'I told you so.' "She's always hated me."

"Now that's not fair. I'm sure there's some logical explanation for all of this," Carl insisted. Both looked at Mariam, still half expecting some perfect excuse leading to a resolution. An elaborate joke, perhaps. But when it became clear that Mariam was serious, that there was no accident, and that the ring had been ruined on purpose, it brought about an uncomfortable ending to the dinner that no one wanted to eat anyway.

Carl's walk terminated in the therapy gardens, empty this time of year except for small ground creatures. The receding snow provided the false promise of spring, but soon enough, it would be hidden beneath a white blanket again. The benches were slick, and an icy rain drifted from the cypresses, their arms reaching back up towards the sky as if a massive weight had been lifted from their shoulders. Carl stood, watching the cypresses, thinking of his own personal burdens that were starting to take a physical toll. They had weakened him, tormented him. He wished they would dissipate, taken by the warmth of a sunny day, away from him forever. Far too long had the pain of this burden inflicted only damage. It was time to face it head-on or resign himself to a life of subsisting off the fragments of insincere love thrown his way. He must do it for Mariam's sake…his own, too…and for anyone else who might make the unfortunate decision to allow this burden into their lives. She would shut him out forever, treat him as though he never existed, just as she had done to his brother, John, all those years ago, but he was ready. Her years were numbered now, and the clock was running out for any reckoning in this lifetime.

Barbara's heart raced as she followed closely behind. It was nearly two o'clock in the morning, and everyone was asleep except for her and Shirley. The two women held their breath as they walked past the nurse's station, relieved to find the nurse on duty fast asleep, her head resting on an extra pillow along the counter. Shirley grabbed a set of keys, carelessly left lying beside her. The hallway contained the sounds of soft snoring coming from behind closed doors, yet the doors to the witches' rooms stood wide open, an eerie vacancy beyond the entryway. What had happened to the three women, they wondered. Had they been discharged, like Regina?

The attic door was loud and heavy and risked exposing them, but they had no choice. They had to know who was there. Shirley pulled the handle slowly, the squeaks quieted by the deliberate patience with which the door was moved. Finally, there was enough room for the two women to squeeze through, both sucking in their stomachs as they inched their way towards the attic stairs. They took an equal amount of care to close the door, ensuring no more than a light tap was audible to anyone who may have awoken, before tiptoeing up to the final door, carefully opening and closing it, and then switching on the main light. It was bright, compared to the dimness of the other halls, and both squinted as they scanned the attic for any signs of life. The floor was dusty, their footprints from the night before still present. The stalls sat empty, and it suddenly occurred to Shirley that neither had even considered the prospect of potentially encountering other patients in isolation, though both understood in their hearts that their location of confinement had been chosen with particular malice. The stalls further down were empty as well. No signs of children or toys or even tiny footprints. Perhaps there had been no one else at all.

Just as the women were ready to admit defeat, Shirley noticed something peculiar sitting on the windowsill, something she was sure had not been there five minutes before, that nearly took the breath right out of her…a teddy bear, old and blue, loved, yet forgotten. There were other items, too…older-model toy cars, a yo-yo, a handful of jacks, playing cards, and a small stack of old-fashioned children's books. Her foot touched something else…a mat, no bigger than a dog's bed, lying on the dirty floor. A sickening feeling hit her in the gut. This had been where a child had stayed, perhaps even lived.

Barbara stared at the sight before her, unsure what to make of it. They looked at each other, too shocked to speak. Barbara took the teddy carefully into her arms, as if cradling a baby, and her hand came across embroidered stitching on the bear's foot…John. What a sad existence it must have been for a child in the attic, much less anywhere in the hospital.

"Mama?" came a small voice. Both women strained their ears. Had they heard what they thought they had? They stood still, their breath shallow, almost silent, listening for anything out of the ordinary.

"Did you hear that?" Shirley asked. Barbara nodded.

"Mama?" an anguished voice repeated. Shirley fell backwards and onto the floor with a loud thump. Her heart pounded through her chest, and any feeling in her extremities not already lost from the cold was lost to fear. She breathed quickly yet got no air and felt as though she might pass out right there on the floor. And just when it seemed it could not get any worse, the lightbulbs overhead burst, scattering glass across the floor. It was dark, very dark. The moonlight cast silver slivers through the windows, barely enough to see anything at all except the soft outline of Barbara's face. She was talking to someone unseen in the darkness.

"Are you John?" Shirley heard her ask.

"Yes," the voice of a young boy answered.

"Why are you here?"

"Mama sent me away when I got sick."

"What happened to you?"

There was quiet. Barbara turned her head to look at the window beside her, as if following another's gaze or pointing of the finger, though Shirley could not tell which, as whatever Barbara saw was visible to her eyes alone.

"How terrible. Was it an accident?"

"We were just playing, Maddie and I. She told me I could fly if I jumped with her."

"Barbara!" Shirley nervously called out after her. "Stop it! What are you doing?" But it seemed as though Barbara could not hear her. The moonlight now illuminated another face and a small hand that ran through Barbara's hair.

"Will you come with me? You could be my mother."

"Barbara!" Shirley grabbed her roommate's shoulders and shook her, yet Barbara did not so much as flinch. Her body was present, but her mind was in another world.

"My poor baby," she cried. Her eyes focused on the boy before her, taking no notice of Shirley. "I'm so sorry."

"Barbara!" Shirley pleaded. "He's not your baby. Wake up!" Yet she did not budge. For a moment, the little boy glowed so brightly that she could see his full figure and the dark clothing he wore. He led Barbara towards the window before fading again into the darkness. Shirley watched helplessly, unable to move. And then there was that horrible scream, the one that would keep her up at night for years to come, the one she could never forget.

"No!" Shirley rushed to the window, suddenly free of whatever had held her back. The wind poured through the lower half, filling the room with fresh air, not much cooler than the attic itself, for the first time in decades. A woman lied sprawled in the grass below, perfectly still, peaceful at last. "Barbara!" she screamed.

The staff below had awoken, and Shirley could hear a crowd of footsteps ascending the stairs. There was nowhere to go, nowhere to hide. She stood and waited for the inevitable discovery and whatever came with it. The heavy door swung open, and a team of nurses, led by Cynthia, burst into the room, drawing robes closed with the sudden change in temperature.

"For goodness' sake. What is the meaning of this?" Cynthia angrily demanded, staring at Shirley in disbelief.

"There was a boy, and Barbara…" Shirley pointed at the window, her finger trembling. Two nurses ran to the window and gasped when they saw Barbara's lifeless body sprawled out in the grass. There was a mad dash of footsteps in the stairwell, followed by the sound of an alarm that Shirley had never heard before ringing out from below. The voices outside grew louder and more frantic. Cynthia closed the window and locked the latch, though Shirley wondered whether the lock would ever do anyone a bit of good.

"What in God's name were you two doing up here?"

"We wanted to find out who else was up here with us last night."

"No one else is here," Cynthia retorted, as if scolding a small child scared of a monster under the bed. But Shirley could tell that there was something Cynthia was hiding. Her eyes gave away what her lips sought to keep secret. She knew there were others, too. "Just look what your explorations have caused," she said, angrily grabbing Shirley's arm and leading her back to her room, past the curious looks of other women in the hall. The door locked securely behind her, leaving only the sound of keys clanking down the hallway and the chaos unfolding outside. From the window, she watched as staff with flashlights ran frantically to and from the area where Barbara fell. Then came the sirens.

Eventually, the activity outside quieted, and everyone else at Chastain Park fell back asleep, but Shirley sat in deafening silence, staring at Barbara's empty bed and the pictures of various relatives that scattered the windowsill. It was her fault. She had been the one to bring up the idea of exploring the attic and had convinced Barbara that they needed to find out who else was up there. By the time the morning medications announcement rang out over the intercom at six o'clock sharp, she had not moved from her one corner of the bed. Her dress was wet from drying tears, and her eyelids felt too heavy to lift.

"Dr. Richter, I am putting my foot down for once. It's just too much."

"Shh," he scolded. "Just a little while longer. I promise."

"Absolutely not. Three in one year is too many. Besides, I've noticed that Nurse Baker is growing suspicious."

"Suspicious? How do you mean?" Dr. Richter seemed more intrigued than worried, despite everything being on the line should certain suspicions ever be confirmed.

"Dr. Richter, really. This is serious." Cynthia's stern face, usually reserved for her patients, was a look he despised. It reminded him of a certain other woman whose intolerable nature he detested.

"How much does she know?"

"Nurse Baker? Well, she notices patterns and has mentioned such specifically to me. She has extensive psychiatric knowledge with experience spanning several other psychiatric hospitals across the nation, and she has questioned the use of various medications on more than one occasion. The death of Ms. Walker has only fed into her suspicious. She has threatened to go to the authorities. It's only a matter of time."

"Are you sure she knows?"

"It is my opinion that she does."

A moment of silence passed while he seemed to consider the predicament before him. As much as he hated to admit it, Cynthia was right on this one. He had to proceed carefully. There was a fine balance he must maintain to keep it all from toppling over.

"You are right," he said reluctantly. "Ask Mr. Jim Benton to meet me in my office immediately, will you?"

"Of course."

A few minutes later, a middle-aged gentleman, balding and unshaven, knocked on Dr. Richter's door. He was a former car mechanic who had killed his girlfriend and two other women over the course of two decades. The state had ruled him mentally unfit to stand trial by means of psychopathy and had determined that the safest route for him, and any potential victims, was institutionalization.

"Mr. Benton, take a seat." Jim did as requested. He wondered why he was seeing the good doctor when it was not his day to do so. "How are you?"

"Well, just fine, I suppose."

"I will be direct. How would you like to regain access to the industry hall?"

"I thought I was kicked out for good after the little incident," he reminded Dr. Richter.

"Yes, I know what was decided. But I've had some time to reconsider and think we could work something out."

"I would like that very much," he nodded. A few years before, he had intentionally set ablaze the kitchen of Francis Hall and, thereafter, had been banned from any further visits to the building. He wondered why he would be given another chance and figured Dr. Richter had a good reason. A brief pause followed, during which both men sat in silence, each understanding that this was some skillful chess move.

"I have a favor to ask of you. Now, it would have to stay just between you and me." He had known Jim for close to a decade now and found him to be a straightforward individual with just enough malleability to be useful in predicaments such as the this. "Do you think you'd be able to do a little brake work on one of the staff's cars? It's an emergency, actually."

"Whatever you want, Doc." Both knew exactly what Dr. Richter meant. He had helped the doctor before on rare occasions and knew to keep his mouth zipped about it.

"Good then. I will remember your generosity, and of course," he motioned his hand, "restore all access to Francis Hall. Which industry profession do you prefer?"

"Butchering."

To that, Dr. Richter gulped. He felt sick to his stomach, but this was his only option, he reminded himself. It had to be done if this major liability risk was to be neutralized.

"Very well. You will begin tomorrow."

"I will get to work then," he said, devoid of any emotion. "Make sure the front doesn't give me any hassle for walking outside."

"You will need these." Dr. Richter handed over shears, pliers, and screwdrivers, reminding Jim to keep them hidden.

Ms. Margaret Baker was a sweet woman in her mid-thirties whom he had gotten on quite well with, and Dr. Richter took no joy in plotting her demise. But he had no choice, he reminded himself. She had stepped into the spider's web, and sometimes, unfortunate things happen.

Chapter Ten

January quickly came and went, and by early February, the ground had been hidden beneath twelve inches of snow for two weeks. The wind seeped through the old windowpanes and howled at night, loudly enough to keep Shirley up. But she did not sleep much these days anyway. Her thoughts were relegated to the sight of Barbara's lifeless body and the children in the attic. She had become a walking zombie, only emerging for meals and her obligatory work in the bakery or, alternatively, meetings with Dr. Richter. When she was not engaged in any of the aforementioned activities, she was kept locked away in her room. The staff would not risk her wandering off again. Her seclusion also eliminated interactions with other patients on the ward and visits to the nurses' station to check for deliveries.

She wondered whether Cheryl had sent any more letters. If the nurses were keeping them, she would never have known. She had sent her old roommate a letter each week. They had started out cheerful and optimistic but had grown more somber as time passed. She wondered whether the staff sent the letters out at all, yet continued to write, hoping that someone would hear her and respond. However, with the lack of response, it was beginning to feel as though she was writing nothing more than diary entries.

Shirley had written all about her friendships with Regina and Barbara and detailed the spontaneous Christmas party thrown by the kind Nurse Robert, who had seemingly disappeared following the event. She wondered what had become of him and was beginning to suspect that he was being kept from her and perhaps anyone else who dared to celebrate at Francis Hall. Later letters detailed living with the crushing guilt of Barbara's death and the isolation that followed as a prisoner in her own room. She had even begun to miss the smell of her cigarettes. Her last letter shared the demise of a nurse, whose car mysteriously sped into a tree on hospital property. Though Shirley had only encountered her a handful of times, she had liked her. Nurse Baker was different than the others….compassionate and patient.

Dr. Richter, once optimistic about releasing her home quickly, now refused to provide any sort of estimate for her discharge, claiming that she was far too ill to even consider life outside of the hospital for the foreseeable future. Life at Chastain Park had become bleak, as had her outlook on life. Some days, she felt worse off than when she arrived and had fleeting thoughts of whether she would be better off dead.

It was a Tuesday afternoon in early March, and Shirley was just finishing up a turkey sandwich and chips before being ushered off to Francis Hall for an afternoon of baking, when a shrill scream came from the main lobby. The chitter chatter of the dining hall quieted as ears perked up, curious about the disruption. A few more bloody murder screams followed, and all eyes turned towards the lobby doorway, curious as to what was happening beyond. The screaming continued.

"I will not. Get your hands off of me!" an older woman yelled at the top of her lungs. "There must be some mistake. Carl, tell them they are mistaken," she demanded.

"Please don't make this more difficult than it has to be," came a calm, cold voice.

"Don't touch me," she warned the staff, who had moved in, surrounding her. "Get away. For God's sake, Carl, do something," she begged, tears welling up in her eyes.

Several staff members grabbed her arms, ushering her away to the administrative offices. Dr. Richter followed quickly behind.

"How could you do this to me?" the woman screamed. "I am your mother!"

The door to the offices slammed shut, and her yells became no more than muffled objections to whatever was taking place. Every eye stared at that door, and the dining hall was filled with whispers, wondering what was going on behind it. Was Dr. Richter really sending his own mother, against her will, to an institution? More likely, it was some deranged patient who only thought she was his mother. Most in the dining hall agreed upon the latter, as it was unfathomable that the good doctor would commit his own mother to the very place he worked. Those who entertained the former were scolded among the groups. What a silly prospect and not a far cry from the notion of letting the insane run the asylum.

That afternoon, Shirley baked eighteen pies and ten loaves of bread. Her arms ached from kneading, and the smell of yeast lingered in her nose, even as she laid down in her bed for the night. It reminded her of cooking with her mother, and of the times she would walk in the door after school to the smell of freshly-baked bread, seasoned with herbs from the garden. But as she reminisced, the smell shifted to a sour, pungent odor, and a queasiness came over her. Her limbs grew cold, and her body shivered. A fear took over. The air vents. In the dimness of the moonlight, a slight, purplish haze of smoke filtered out, dissipating over Barbara's bed. And then a thought crept in she never expected to have in a place meant to keep her safe. Was her air being poisoned? Were they trying to gas her? Instinctively, she grabbed Barbara's bedding and stuffed bits of sheeting between each of the vent openings. The haze slowed to a small trickle around the edges, and almost instantaneously, her body warmed and the nausea ceased.

For several weeks now, she had suspected the staff had been trying to poison her. But this was the first time they had used the vents. Perhaps they feared Barbara's story might get out to the press…or that Shirley would tell local newspapers about her inhumane isolation in the attic as punishment for a harmless Christmas party. What horrible publicity, not to mention the threat of a potential site visit by regulators. No, they could not have that.

She had stopped drinking the milk after a glass turned her stomach sour and had given up the meat casserole when she noticed remnants of a crushed pill inside. She carefully watched what others chose in the dining hall and ate only what they did, avoiding some of her usual and unpopular favorites like the plague. She no longer wore her own clothes, afraid that they had been washed with rodent repellent or other toxins, opting instead for Barbara's. On laundry days, she sent her own clean clothes down to be washed, as if they had been worn, and re-wore Barbara's clothing. She did not know how much longer she could hide the flour spills or body odor and knew that sooner or later, Cynthia would discover that she was not changing her clothes.

Shirley had stopped washing her hair for the same reason, afraid that shampoo bottles were being switched out prior to her showers with chemical-laden substitutes. She brushed her teeth but only with water, and her breath had a strong, rancid odor. Her skin was dry and cracked from the bitter cold, yet she refused all lotions. Anything in a tube or bottle could be easily tainted with poison. She was safe nowhere, and they would stop at nothing to silence her.

The sound of the morning alarm jolted Shirley out of a light sleep, and the jingle of Cynthia's keys grew louder as she moved from room to room. There was a quick knock, and the door swung open. A tray bore the usual concoction of medications. There were the small white and large gray pills, followed by two brownish tablets and a yellow pill. Weeks prior, the pink pill had inexplicably disappeared and was replaced by the yellow. Shirley had wanted to ask about the change but caught herself, sure that no good would come of such an attempt at answers.

"When did you last shower?" Cynthia asked, staring at Shirley's stringy, oily hair.

"Last night," she lied.

"It looks as though your hair could use a good lathering. See to it that you wash your hair this evening." She glanced at the young woman up and down. "And change your dress at once. It looks absolutely filthy," she scolded. "You will be getting a new roommate this afternoon, so please see to it," she said, grabbing Barbara's sheets from the air vent, "that you keep the room in order." She bent over to make the bed.

"Who is she?"

"That is nothing for you to trouble yourself over." Cynthia straightened out the duvet. "You will find out soon enough."

That afternoon, Shirley sat in Dr. Richter's office. She had been waiting for nearly a half hour for their session to begin, but the doctor was nowhere to be seen. She relaxed her feet on the coffee table and quickly lowered them, chiding herself for her poor manners, before standing up to stretch. Had the doctor forgotten? Or perhaps something unexpected had come up.

Her finger ran across the collection of psychiatric books displayed on the bookshelf, smooth against the back of her finger, their titles illuminated by the grayish winter light that filtered through the window, before stopping on one that caught her eye. It was smaller than the other thick medical books, its height no bigger than her hand, and resembled a pocket guide. On the cover of a nondescript red and black cover sat the gold-etched words, *Fear Triggers*. Something about it drew her in, and she flipped through the book, indiscriminately stopping on page twenty-five.

...upon the quality of nurses housed within the facility. They must have the highest fortitude and ability yet possess the innate skill to distance themselves emotionally. When you find one of such quality, you must retain them by whatever means necessary, for they are your base and support, without which you will find yourself highly unsuccessful in your endeavors.

Pick your patients with ruthless discrepancy. Just as your nurse must be a perfect fit, so too must those...

The sound of footsteps startled her, and she quickly tossed the odd book back onto the shelf, exactly where she had found it. The door remained closed, but the muffled whispers of a rather heated argument seeped through, undeterred. Though the nature of the conversation could not be deciphered, the voices of Dr. Richter and Cynthia were distinguishable. She wondered what they were fighting about. Was it her? Had she done something else to anger the powers that be? The voices stopped, and she rushed back to her seat just in time before Dr. Richter entered, apologizing for his tardiness, blaming it on a patient emergency. A single bead of sweat on his brow was the only remaining evidence of the argument that had taken place moments before.

"Ms. Fitzpatrick, how have things been going the last few days?" Dr. Richter studied her for a moment, one might say with a certain amusement in his eyes, noting her unkempt hair and filthy dress. The smell of body odor permeated the air. He found the shift fascinating and wanted to know more about what drove her towards this sudden disregard for hygiene.

"Just fine, I guess," Shirley lied. She had decided from the first day that she would limit any confessions that might delay her discharge. But as months passed, and her condition, by all accounts, worsened, she felt herself in a constant state of coverup, for if they found out what was really going on inside her head, she would surely become a permanent resident. Her only hope of ever leaving was to lie, to act like everything was normal, even when it so clearly was not.

"How would you say you are coping with the loss of your roommate, Barbara?"

Shirley's sleep consisted of occasional catnaps here and there. Her thoughts brought her back to that night, that horrible night, and seeing her lifeless body on the ground…a night that, if given the opportunity to take back and do over, she would in an instant. "I guess as well as can be expected."

"Cynthia tells me that you have been covering your vents with sheets. Why is that, especially with the cold weather we've had?" His pen swirled and then dangled loosely from his fingertips. Just when Shirley thought he would drop it, he grasped his fingers around it tightly and made a quick note in his notebook.

"Well, I guess my room has been warm," she lied. "I've awoken several nights drenched in sweat." She was not about to tell him the real reason.

"Cynthia has told me that your room actually feels quite chilly, that when she enters in the mornings, the windows have been frosted on the inside." He cleared his throat. "Are you certain there is nothing else you wish to tell me?"

At this point, she felt sure Dr. Richter knew her excuse was a lie. But she was not going to give him an inch. They would never let her leave if they knew she believed her air and food were being poisoned by the very people entrusted with her care…or that the boy in the attic was real.

"Only that I don't appreciate being kept locked in my room like a prisoner. I want to leave. I am better now and have personal matters to attend to." The urgency in her voice dropped to a soft pleading. "When may I go home?"

"Go home?" Dr. Richter seemed shocked by the mere mention of something so preposterous. "My dear, you simply are not well enough for the outside world. You require constant care. You belong here."

Shirley could not believe what she was hearing. It had been nearly three months when she had expected to be home within weeks.

"You don't understand. I can't stay here. I still have to settle my parents' estate. There's no one else who can do this. And there's school…I'm supposed to graduate in May. I have classes to finish for that to happen. I *am* better. Please let me go," she begged. Her heart raced. She felt trapped, like a wild animal in a cage, desperate for freedom. "I don't want to obtain an attorney, but I will if I need to."

"That is precisely why you must stay. The world will not solve your problems. It will only add to them. And if you want to tell yourself that you are fully better, you are only fooling yourself. When was the last time you showered, changed your clothes, ate something? Your weight check yesterday indicates that you've dropped nearly ten pounds over the past month. I'd say that's concerning, and I'm willing to bet any judge, should they even take the case of a woman in your position, would agree with me."

"I should like to use the phone," she stated stubbornly.

"You may do so at the discretion of the nurses."

A moment of silence followed. The room held an uncomfortable tension in the air and felt as though it might explode at any time. There was something else Shirley needed to talk about, though she knew bringing it up risked adding to Dr. Richter's case against her. Still, she had to know.

"I have written to Cheryl, my roommate back at school, every week and heard nothing in return. It would be most unlike her to ignore my correspondences. I believe the nurses are either not sending my letters or not delivering hers." The words were out. Too late. She stared at the doctor with a cold stare, instantly sorry she had asked. It was clear that Dr. Richter was none too pleased to have the stolen care package fiasco possibly play out a second time.

"I highly doubt that the nurses would do anything of the sort, but I will look into the matter if you insist. I shall let you know if I discover anything untoward, though I must reiterate that I don't expect that to be the case. I think you will find the nurses, if you would only give them the benefit of the doubt, to be on your side. They want to help you, and taking your letters would not be productive towards the shared goal of getting better, would it?" His answer was a small concession in her favor, perhaps meant as a bridge towards improving the souring doctor-patient relationship.

"No, but I'd appreciate it being looked into anyhow."

"Very well."

After the meeting concluded, Shirley spent the remainder of the day locked in her room, leaving only briefly for dinner. She found herself questioning whether it was worth hiding her paranoia or anything else that might be perceived as a sign of mental illness. What did it really matter if she was stuck in there anyway? Perhaps Dr. Richter was right, and she, in some sort of delusional state, was just in denial. Maybe she had gone crazy.

Before going to sleep, she took one of her freshly cleaned uniforms and stuffed it into the air vent. Then she donned one of Barbara's filthy nightgowns, ran a comb through her greasy hair, and tucked herself in tight, preparing for a night of bitter coldness in the room without heat.

It was several hours later when the unfamiliar sound of snoring jostled her out of dreamland. It reverberated off the walls, creating an echo chamber around her. She tried to ignore it and buried her head in her pillow to no avail. Perhaps the intercom had inadvertently been left on, capturing the snoring of a sleeping nurse down the hall and casting it into every room off the hallway. Or was it coming from next door, the result of her neighbor's awful head cold? She listened with her ear pressed against the wall for a moment before deciding that was not the case. Then, a snore so loud that it seemed to rattle the bedframe rang out like some sort of inhumane alarm bell. She was certain it had come from Barbara's bed. With great trepidation, she tiptoed across the room and noticed, somewhat horrified, the S-shaped form of a person under the sheets. She jumped backwards, and then, after catching her breath, slowly pulled back the covers. She suddenly realized that the person before her was the new roommate she had been told about, the crazy woman from the lobby. How long had she been there? Shirley was certain she had not been present when she had fallen asleep.

The woman was older with grayish-white hair and wore a nightgown identical to Shirley's. Drool spilled from her mouth onto the pillow. The snoring continued on, the new patient completely oblivious to her presence.

"Excuse me." Shirley gently nudged the woman before her. "I'm sorry, excuse me." She nudged once more, but the woman did not even flinch. In fact, the snoring seemed to grow louder. Feeling defeated, she made her way back to her own bed, begrudgingly burying her head under the pillow. But covering the ears did little to quell the intermittent rattling of objects that accompanied her new roommate's breathing.

Early the next morning, Cynthia entered with her usual cocktail. She set down the tray and rubbed her arms for warmth. Her breath hung in a mist before her. The windows had iced along the inside, too. She wasted no time in pulling the dress from the vent, and a burst of heat flowed through the room, filling every corner with warmth. Shirley looked away, unwilling to meet the irritated gaze that had been shot in her direction. The dress would be replaced as soon as Cynthia left. Shirley only hoped the room would not become too saturated with poisonous chemicals in the meantime.

Fear of another reprimand had her downing the white and gray pills, the brown tablets, and the new yellow pill without questions or complaints. As she took the final pill, Shirley could not help but notice that Cynthia looked away, just for a moment, but long enough to give her pause. Was Cynthia hiding something? Were the pills poisoned, too? The medication tray made its way over to Barbara's bed. The new roommate did not awaken as Cynthia lifted the heavy, wrinkled arm and injected a syringe. The woman slept as though nothing had happened, snoring away within the dreamscape of another world. Shirley could see the woman's hair, peering over the edge of the covers that kept her face hidden from view, and envied her ability to sleep in this wretched place. She would give anything to escape this hellhole, even if just in her mind.

"Who is she?" Shirley finally asked.

"Her name is Ruth." And without further explanation, Cynthia left the room, locking the women in behind.

Several days would pass before the mysterious woman awoke, and by the time the last dose of sedatives had worn off, her bedsheets were soaked in urine and reeked of feces. At last, one of the nurses changed her bedding and helped her into the shower. The hospital was filled with whispers that she was related to Dr. Richter, though at Chastain Park, one rumor was as good as the next, and most patients found themselves dismissing the idea as idle gossip.

It was four days after her arrival before Ruth finally appeared before the curious at breakfast. Some gawked at her, unabashedly staring with gaping mouths, while others nonchalantly glanced in her direction from time to time. Whether or not the rumors were true, they had the unintended effect of building interest around the new woman.

Together, she and Shirley were quite the sight to behold. Shirley's appearance continued to worsen. Her greasy hair had begun to thin, yielding large bald spots along the top and side of her head. Yet she hardly noticed the clumps of brown hair on her pillow. She had become accustomed to brushing it with the sweep of her hand onto the floor, giving it as much thought as shooing away a fly. Her clothing, unwashed and with a strong stench of body odor, hung several sizes too large from her thinning frame. The other patients stayed away, and she could not blame them.

Ruth chose cooked oatmeal, and Shirley followed suit, despite her dislike of the cereal. But she would watch the older woman eat it first and make sure she did not become ill. Only then could she rest assured that the food was safe for consumption. By the end of breakfast, she had taken only a few bites, matching Ruth's intake. Her meals had become barely sufficient. Soon, she would have to find a way to leave the hospital if she was going to survive. Dr. Richter seemed to have no plans of allowing that to happen, and for the first time, she began to seriously contemplate an escape plan.

Ruth said nothing during breakfast. In fact, she had not uttered a single word to anyone. She stared off into to space, unresponsive to any attempt at conversation. Shirley wondered whether she was mentally disabled. Perhaps her family had cared for her, and now, in her old age, they no longer could. It was quite possible that her family was deceased, and there was simply no one left. She felt sorry for her.

Later that afternoon, as the other women in the hall were shuffled downstairs for visitation with family, the two women sat silently in their respective beds. Ruth did not complain when Shirley replaced the gown over the air vent or of the stench of body odor that enveloped the entire room. Every now and then, Shirley could hear her muttering indistinguishable words to herself, and when she became too loud, Cynthia rushed in with a syringe of medication, putting her into a deep sleep that she did not awake from until the next morning.

Chapter Eleven

Sunday morning began like any other. Cynthia emerged right on schedule, holding her silver tray of medications. She handed over the small white and large grayish pills, followed by the two brownish tablets, and finally, the yellow pill that had recently become a staple in her regimen.

Ruth's insufferable snoring had kept Shirley awake most of the night. She sat up in bed, appearing well-rested and oblivious to the torture she inflicted upon her roommate. Her legs hung over the side of the bed, and she swung them back and forth like a fidgety child. Cynthia watched for a second, contemplating whether or not to intervene, before taking the small cup of water from Shirley's hands. Seconds later, an indecipherable gibberish flowed from across the room, and once again, all attention was focused on Ruth.

"The car swampooned, oh jeez, quick to the ground. I'll say, that dirty dopper!" And then, the words, "My son, Carl," slipped clearly and undeniably from the lips of the old woman. Until now, she had barely uttered two words, but suddenly, she was revealing names. With a syringe in hand, Cynthia rushed over to the bed and pushed the needle deep into the woman's arm, sending her back into an immediate slumber. The room returned to the calm repetition of snoring, combined with the huffing of a woman badly out of shape. Cynthia sat down at the end of Ruth's bed to catch her breath, deep in thought about the unexpected utterings of her patient. Something would have to be done and quickly. She would discuss the incident with Dr. Richter right away.

The abrupt distraction provided the golden opportunity that Shirley had waited for. She quietly turned towards the wall and spit the pills out into one big, sloppy mess, quickly stuffing the evidence under her pillow and out of sight. Cynthia was still so frazzled that she neglected to notice and, for the first time, left the vent covering untouched. She grabbed the tray and rushed out the door, locking it tightly behind her.

Shirley could hear her voice on the other side…and Dr. Richter's, too. It reminded her of that day she had waited so long to see him in his office. They spoke in whispers, trying to avoid being overheard. Shirley tiptoed towards the door, longing…needing…to know what they were saying, and once she got within two feet, could make out most of their conversation.

"We can't leave her like this. Running in every time she starts talking is taking away from my other duties. It's wearing on me. She's a liability. You've got to do it."

"That's my mother."

"Precisely my point. You do understand what will happen if you keep putting it off?"

The doctor grunted. He did not care for the obvious reminder.

"Some of the patients already suspect. Just imagine what she might say if I can't get in there quickly enough."

"Is Ms. Fitzpatrick aware?"

"No, I don't believe so."

"Let's keep it that way. Alright, this morning then, seven o'clock."

Cynthia breathed an audible sigh of relief. "Very good. I'll ensure she's ready, doctor."

Shirley scurried back to her bed, knowing all too well the punishment that would follow for eavesdropping. Ruth was still fast asleep when Cynthia returned a few minutes later to bring Shirley down to breakfast. In the dining hall, she nibbled on toast and eggs, and when the woman across the table stopped eating hers, she followed suit. That was the rule she had made for herself. Whatever the others ate, she ate, and when they stopped eating, she stopped. It lessened the risk, should the food, in fact, have been tainted.

When she returned just after seven, Ruth's bed was already empty. The old woman reemerged within a half hour on a stretcher, still snoring, but there was something different about her. Shirley waited until the staff left and it was just the two of them to take a closer look. It was as if she was looking into the face of Regina. Her eye sockets were bruised, and suddenly, she understood what they had done to her. They wanted to erase her memory, to turn her into a shell of a person, one whose malleable mind could be controlled and, most importantly, revealed no secrets.

Shirley became more skilled in the art of pill hiding. Each morning, she lodged one after another under her tongue and had even mastered drinking water while holding the pills in place. As soon as Cynthia turned her back, she would spit them out and hide them under her pillow until she could flush them down the toilet. Without the pills came clarity of mind. A gradual dissipation of paranoia ensued, washed away from her psyche like the recession of a wave, coming and going at first, until it completely disappeared. She told no one, for she knew they wanted to keep her ill.

Her body was malnourished and tired. She longed to eat a large meal without fear of poisoning but carefully limited herself, fully aware that any significant changes would serve as a red flag. She continued to avoid basic hygiene measures and wore the same filthy clothes, which reeked of an unholy mixture of body odor, flour, and dirt. Every morning, Cynthia removed the dress covering the vent, and Shirley replaced it. The cold felt ever more piercing, yet she fought the urge to deviate from old habits. Her apparent struggles seemed to please the good doctor and his assistant, as the pill regimen remained exactly the same. A sick patient is what they wanted, and a sick patient she would give them.

Every few days, Ruth was taken away for the brief procedure that left her eyes perpetually surrounded by darkness. She required fewer and fewer injections, for the procedure itself kept her in a stupor. She spoke to no one and mentioned no names. In fact, she did not seem to recognize Dr. Richter at all. He was a stranger to her, for all anyone could tell, and if not for the very occasional stares of longing, which one might expect from a mother missing her child, no one would ever be the wiser. But Shirley knew. She would never forget that Ruth had called him her son. She noticed the fear in Dr. Richter's eyes when Ruth had violent outbursts, hitting and yelling unintelligible words at anyone around. She noticed, too, a sadness when she no longer remembered him. And she observed a certain inhumane thrill in his eyes on the nights that he and Cynthia medicated her and lugged her limp body out of the room. Shirley wondered where they took her so late in the evening. One to two hours of quiet would pass as the patients on the floor settled into bed for the evening, and around midnight, the sound of distant screaming would awaken many, though they dared not complain for fear of retaliation. This would go on for hours until it presumably became too much, even for the doctor and his nurse, and by morning, Ruth would be back in her bed, snoring, as if nothing had happened at all.

Shirley wondered what she endured at their hands when no one was looking. But whatever their secrets harbored, Ruth was unable to share. She slept most of the day, except for meals, and when awake, stared off into space, unresponsive to the outside world. It was as though she was a body absent of soul and mind, living and breathing yet already dead inside.

Shirley studied the woman as she slept. She had the same nose as Dr. Richter, pointed and slightly upturned near the tip. The shape of her eyes bore a striking resemblance to the doctor's as well, although his were brown and hers blue. Though Ruth no longer communicated verbally, Shirley could not help but notice a tensing of her body that radiated down to her fingertips whenever he entered the room. Her eyes would stare, and her mouth would widen, yet only primal sounds emerged. She was afraid of him.

Shirley felt sorry for the old woman. It was clear to her that she was being mistreated and possibly even abused. On days that she was not required to work over at Francis Hall, baking the afternoons away, she adopted a new hobby, acting as a comforter to her. She would scoot the room's lone chair over to her bedside and hold her hand, telling her stories of her own life before institutionalization. She spoke of her parents and their deaths and of her many projects back at the sorority. She talked about teaching and her former fiancé, Sean Mackey. Ruth looked at her sometimes, and every now and then, it seemed as though she understood.

One morning, the yellow pill was inexplicably removed from Shirley's medication regimen, gone without any explanation other than it was the good doctor's orders. To be given in its place was a slightly smaller tablet, round and dark red, bearing resemblance to a stray polka dot. Though Shirley would have paid a pretty penny to find out why the change was made, she knew enough not to ask. As per usual, she hid the medications underneath her tongue and then spit them out as soon as the door locked behind her. Ruth watched from across the room, a silent witness to her noncompliance, incapable of telling a soul even if she wanted to.

The wet glob of pills sat in a sloppy mess in her hand, some dissolving at the edges. Shirley studied the pills, undeterred by Ruth's blank stare, and contemplated the unexpected decision that stood before her. She could take the red tablet for a short time in order to learn and then act out its side effects, eliminating any possible suspicions of medicinal noncompliance. Or she could immediately discard the tablet and, not knowing the side effects, act as though it had no impact on her at all. If she chose the latter, Dr. Richter might up the dosage or, more concerningly, request injections, which she could not escape. She decided upon the former as the safest route to proceed. She popped the soggy red tablet back into her mouth and begrudgingly swallowed. A bitter taste lingered afterwards, a flavor that could only be described as a peppery, lemony combination, so pungent that she nearly gagged.

With the cessation of the yellow pill, it became vital to act as though the side effects of the medication were waning. Shirley began to wash her hair, and the stringiness was replaced with a fullness that, at least partially, covered areas of alopecia that had become prominent in recent months. She ate vigorously, denying herself nothing and filling her stomach until it felt like it just might pop. She washed and changed her clothing, taking special care to apply deodorant, much to the appreciation of those she encountered. And the nightgown that covered her room's vent and source of heat for so long came down one last time. During therapy sessions, Dr. Richter commended her weight gain and renewed interest in personal hygiene and followed up with questions related to fears and anxieties and any possible hallucinations.

For the first time in months, Shirley felt normalcy in her life. She even found herself questioning malevolence in the medication regimen, chalking her suspicions up to stress and fatigue. But any peace derived from feeling better was short lived.

A few nights later, Shirley abruptly sat up in bed, jolted awake by a voice that she longed for like no other, a voice she knew as well as her own. She opened her eyes, straining to see where it came from. Ruth snored loudly, and for a moment, she thought she had conflated the two sounds. Then she heard it again. This time, the voice called her name so clearly that it could not be denied.

"Mother?" she called out in a whisper, looking nervously around the room. There was only silence, followed by confusion. Had she really heard what she thought she had? The incident replayed in her mind. She was certain someone *had* called her by name and that the voice was that of her mother. But it was impossible. She felt silly for even entertaining the notion. But then, who was it? Shirley covered her body tightly in her sheets, caught in the uncomfortable predicament of not wanting to go back to sleep but being unwilling to seek out what called her either. At some point during the night, she succumbed to fatigue and awoke the next morning, wondering whether it had all been a dream.

Several nights later, just as her thoughts melted away and her mind drifted into sleep, the voice returned. It called her name softly in her ear, and she felt someone holding her hand. She lied stiffly, eyes clinched shut, too afraid to move and quietly begging for it to leave her alone. She opened one eye, hoping to see nothing but the outline of the beds, dresser, and chair in the moonlight, but there was something else…a woman. Though her face was dark, a soft, white glow illuminated an apron of unmistakable familiarity.

"Oh, Mother," Shirley began to weep. "Is that really you?"

"Yes, darling. I'm terribly sorry for what has happened." She squeezed Shirley tight. "You must know that your father and I are okay."

"I've missed you so much. Please stay with me."

"I can't," the voice quivered. "I love you." The words trailed off as she seemingly vanished.

Shirley felt a sense of tranquility after the visit, and when Janet Fitzpatrick reappeared a few nights later, she was no longer afraid. They talked about the crash, which she assured Shirley had been quick and painless. Her parents had not even realized the plane was in dire straits until seconds before impact. She further emphasized that they were at peace and did not want Shirley to suffer because of an unfortunate accident. For the first time since that awful night in October, Shirley felt that everything would be okay.

She was, in fact, so relieved to see her mother that she hesitated to question the sudden onset of visits. The timing was merely a coincidence, she convinced herself. Yet the fact that the mysterious side effect of the red tablet had yet to be revealed was beginning to worry her.

One night, deep within the darkest hours of the night, Janet sat beside Shirley on the bed, gently rubbing her back as she slept, just as she had done when she was a youngster. Shirley was comforted by her presence and no longer feared the ghostly apparition.

"Hi, darling," she began.

"Mother," Shirley responded, sitting up. "I want to see you better." She stroked her mother's soft cheek with her hand, yet the darkness of the room hid most of her features. "Why do you only come at night?"

"So that others will not see me." She gestured towards Ruth.

"Ruth wouldn't tell anyone. I promise. Please let me see you."

"No, you may not." Her words were stern, final, as if she had expected and prepared for this moment. Yet something within Shirley longed so desperately to see the woman who birthed and raised her.

"Is it the injuries you don't want me to see? Is that it? I don't mind. I just want to see you."

"I told you no!" she snapped, her voice deepening into a growl that sent Shirley's heart racing. "You bitch. It's not good enough that I come to visit, is it?" she snarled.

Shirley stared at her mother in shock. She had never heard her curse at anyone before.

"Mother, I…I'm sorry," Shirley stuttered, struggling to find right words. She looked more closely at the apron her mother wore. It had been a gift from her grandmother years ago. The hand-painted flowers and embroidered name 'Janet' looked the same as she remembered, only the person wearing the apron seemed different.

"You were always a pain in the ass." Her voice grew deeper, into a tone that Shirley did not recognize. "I hated you from the minute you were born!" Janet picked up the bedside chair, throwing it with inhuman strength across the room. Shirley could not speak. Who was this woman? It most certainly was not her mother. And as if answering her thoughts, she caught a glimpse of her face in the moonlight. The softness of her cheeks had transformed into a scaly, green leather akin to a crocodile. The eyes were dark and hollow. The hair hung from a balding scalp in thin clumps. It bared teeth impossibly large for its mouth and seemed to have grown several feet taller, its head nearly touching the ceiling. It looked down at her angrily, and Shirley screamed loud enough to alert the nightshift. A team of nurses rushed to the door, taking only seconds to unlock it, but by the time the light was flipped on, it had vanished into the far corner behind Ruth's bed.

"What in God's name, child?" came the voice of an older nurse, hands placed sternly on her hips.

Before Shirley could stop herself, the words spilled from her mouth. "There's a monster in here!" Her finger pointed at the corner, where nothing remained, at least that anyone could see. The nurses looked at each other, failing to understand.

"There's nothing here. Just Ruth," a younger nurse responded, confused. Ruth sat up and looked around, bewildered, trying to comprehend what was going on.

"No, there was a monster!" she insisted, her eyes pleading for someone to believe her.

"It was just a bad dream. Get back to sleep." She led Shirley back to bed and pulled the covers up over her.

Cynthia watched the commotion from the doorway, silently chiding the good doctor. He had gone too far this time. She had warned him. He was going to ruin it for both of them if he was not careful. Her eyes studied the young patient for a moment, wondering whether she knew anything. Some days, she felt in her gut that Shirley knew about the pills and what they were doing to her, but the primal fear in her eyes that night reassured her that she was blissfully unaware. She hoped it would stay that way and that the situation would not necessitate any further unfortunate patient outcomes. Despite her misgivings, Cynthia exited the room with a pep in her step and excitement in her heart, eager to convey the night's events to the doctor first thing in the morning.

From then on, Shirley discarded the red tablet with the others. It had been the biggest lie yet, taking advantage of her rawest vulnerabilities, and for that, she was extremely angry, though she could never let them know. Now, more than ever, she had to keep up the act of compliant and oblivious patient to avoid being deemed a liability risk like the others. She could not let them know that she understood. But maintaining the facade of sick patient meant sharing stories of these nightly encounters with Dr. Richter, even after they subsided, which tugged at her heartstrings far more than she anticipated. Until she could find a way out of Chastain Park, she was checkmated and stuck playing their filthy game.

It was a Thursday afternoon. Francis Hall, usually filled with the hustle and bustle of seamstresses, shoe makers, mattress makers, artists, and bakers, was unusually quiet. That week, a stomach virus had made its rounds through the hospital, capturing patients and staff alike in its path. Shirley had somehow managed to avoid the illness, even after Ruth became sick in the middle of the night and vomited all over the floor, and was one of only four patients available to work in the industry hall that day.

She had just finished pulling six cookie sheets of white chocolate-chip and walnut cookies from the oven when Robert, the nurse who had thrown the notorious surprise Christmas party back in December, emerged in the doorway. She had not seen him since that day and was quite certain it had been decided by the higherups that their paths were not to cross. He looked at her, running his hand nervously through his slicked-back blonde hair, and she stared back, wondering what trouble he might bring this time.

"Hi," he uttered with an embarrassed half-wave. "That smells delicious."

"It's chocolate-chip and walnut cookies. I'm just about to start cinnamon rolls." She wiped her hands on her flour-covered apron. "It's been a while, hasn't it?"

"Yeah. It seems my Christmas party was not looked favorably upon," he chuckled. "I'm sorry you got in trouble for it, too," he said solemnly. "I heard about the attic, and I just think that's awful."

"It's alright. I understand you had no intention of causing a problem. It's not your fault."

"Listen, there's something that I need to talk to you about. Do you mind if we sit?"

"Of course."

The two sat down at the same small table that she and Barbara once shared, divulging their darkest secrets. It was rare that she had time to sit at Francis Hall, and she had almost forgotten the table existed.

Robert looked serious. "I'll be frank. I'm only here today because Nurse Henry," he glanced up towards the floor above, "allowed me to slip in for a minute. Dr. Richter has forbidden me to be around anyone who attended the Christmas party, as I'm sure you've gathered by now." He took a long breath and sighed. "I believe you are in eminent danger."

"In danger? Of what?"

"Dr. Richter…and this place. It has a habit of bringing out the worst in people." He looked around, making sure no one was within earshot.

It was strangely comforting to hear someone else say what she already suspected. In a low voice, she responded, "I already know. He's been ordering pills that make me see and hear things. I've seen snakes that are not there, my deceased mother, too, and believed I was being poisoned for a time. I've also encountered a little boy named John in the attic. For so long, I thought I was going crazy." Robert looked shocked that she knew so much, as if he had expected to have much more convincing to do.

"If you don't mind my asking, how did you figure out that Dr. Richter was manipulating your pills?"

"I stopped taking them, and the hallucinations stopped," she shrugged.

"Unfortunately, there's more," he continued. "Do you remember the death of Nurse Margaret Baker back in January?"

"Of course. How tragic. I heard that she hit an ice patch and skidded into a tree."

"Yes, well, that's the story they want you to believe, anyway. To say that I'm suspicious of the manner of her death is to put it mildly. I was one of the first to arrive at the accident site that day. It was maybe fifty yards or so from the front steps of the hospital. As I approached the automobile, I couldn't help but notice the absence of skid marks in the snow. It was as though she drove full speed directly into the tree, never applying the brakes at all. Even stranger was the fact that her emergency brake had been pulled, which tells me that she tried her best to stop but that the brakes just did not engage. I wanted to do a little investigating, so I visited the parking space she always used. Sure enough, there were several screws lying in the snow, like someone had been working on the car in that spot. I decided to keep my mouth shut about it until I better understood what was going on."

Shirley listened patiently. The handful of others in the building toiled away upstairs, oblivious to the conversation in the kitchen.

"I went to the funeral, and Margaret's sister and I ended up having a long conversation that ran well into the evening. She told me that her sister was convinced that Dr. Richter was conducting experiments on patients using unregulated drugs, an endeavor that posed a serious offense if discovered. Margaret apparently had an expansive work history and strong knowledge of psychiatric medications used outside of Chastain Park. When she brought up concerns to supervising nurses, she was disregarded. When she persisted, she was retaliated against. At one point, Cynthia told her that if she dared to even suggest such a gross malpractice of medicine again, she would be relieved of her duties. It was a short time later that the accident occurred."

"You don't think that…" Shirley pondered.

Robert looked around to make sure no prying ears heard what he had to say. "It's one strange coincidence. I knew I had to figure out what was going on. Dr. Richter has been out sick the past few days, so I snuck into his office to look for any evidence that might corroborate my suspicions. I found this." He held up a thick journal, bound in brown leather, its pages discolored at the edges. Shirley immediately recognized it as the doctor's and the one he scribbled in during each of Shirley's visits. "It seems as though he has a habit of picking women to suffer through his sadistic regimens, and he specifically chooses those with no family around to interfere."

"That's awful," Shirley gasped. "But why?"

"I believe it has something to do with his mother. He writes of her frequently in the journal and describes wanting to confront her on certain matters but being unable to overcome her overbearing personality. So, instead, he takes it out on other females. I think he sees these female patients as versions of his own mother that he can punish for the perceived harm he incurred. It's interesting you mentioned the young boy, John, because..." He opened to a page dated June 8, 1951:

She refuses to acknowledge any wrongdoing in John's care. That narcissistic bitch just left him in the attic to wither away until he had no choice but to jump. Her reliance on reputation prevented her from calling him her son, and rather than nurturing him, she fought so that no one in the outside world might know of his existence. What would the neighbors think if she had a son with epilepsy?

"I spoke with Nurse Geraldine, who has been here for fifty years, at least, and remembers John well. As a boy, Dr. Richter and his father visited him on occasion. His mother, Ruth, never came to see him. Quite a sad story, really."

"How awful. No wonder he has a strained relationship with his mother. Is that why I've been receiving these strange pills? Because he wants to punish me in the way he wishes he could punish his mother?"

"Yes, I believe so. He sees you as a version of her, someone he can punish in her stead to the extent that he begins to feel relief. He has begun to merge his perception of you with that of his mother. It's very dangerous." He turned the journal to another page dated March 17, 1954.

Oh, how I have relished in Ms. Fitzpatrick's recollections of her deceased mother and the utter fear she experiences when "the monster" appears. I find it increasingly difficult to contain my enjoyment of her paranoia. However, Nurse Cynthia has confided that she suspects the patient knows more than she lets on. Therefore, I am forced to bring all pill trials to conclusion. I will schedule a lobotomy for next week and continue with one to two per week until a subdued baseline mental state is reached and any incriminating information gathered is forgotten.

"He's planning to do lobotomies on me?" Shirley asked louder than expected. She stood up, and her chair hit the wall with a bang.

"Shh," Robert scolded. "We can't let anyone else know. At least, not yet. No one," he reiterated.

"But they can't do this to me," she cried. "Please, help me to get out. I can't stay here."

"Okay," he responded, much to her surprise. "It's not going to be easy, but I will get you out. You're going to have to listen to me carefully and do exactly as I say. Do you think you can do that?" He studied Shirley intently, hoping he had not made a massive mistake. Once he helped her, there was no going back. He was prepared to give up the job he had once loved and to leave behind those he could not help, at least not at the moment. But Shirley needed him if there was any hope of a normal existence outside of Chastain Park, and they were running out of time. He would figure out the financial implications of his decision later. He had stashed away a small fortune…two thousand dollars…over the years, and that would be enough to get by on for a while.

"Yes, I can," Shirley replied confidently and noticed a sigh of relief in his face as the words hit his ears.

"Very good then. I will leave detailed instructions under your door tonight. Please make sure to keep an eye out for them because if they fall into the wrong hands…" He did not need to finish. Both understood that should their escape plan be discovered, mercy would be in short supply.

"Okay," Shirley said trembling. She was going to get out. It was finally happening. Never in her life had she been so relieved and frightened simultaneously.

"You must tell no one. Carry on with your day as if all is normal. Eat dinner, shower, dress for bed…do all the things you normally would. It is vital that you don't set off any alarms."

She took a deep breath, and Robert placed his hand on hers.

"It's going to be okay. Just trust me."

Chapter Twelve

Dear Shirley,

I will arrive at your room at 2:00 a.m. sharp. Prior to my arrival, you are to do the following tasks:

1. Pen the following note on scratch paper:
"Please do not disturb. I have been ill all evening."

2. Ensure all lights in the room are off.

3. Change into your daytime attire. You are to carry your shoes until we exit the building.

4. Gather only small, personal possessions you can wear or easily carry. All else must be left behind.

5. Stuff pillows under the sheets to look as though you are sleeping beneath.

6. Leave the note beside the bed so it will be visible to staff who enter.

Once I arrive, stay close by my side. We will not have time to talk. You must trust me. I cannot divulge the entirety of the plan until we are in the clear.

-R.P.

The letter had been slipped beneath the door just after nine, its writing nervously scribbled on torn spiral notebook paper. A panic set in with the realization that hours from now, she would be making a daring escape. She had done exactly as Robert had asked and carried on normal conversations with other patients in the dining hall, eaten a full dinner, and then showered and dressed for bed. Every part of the day had been just like any other, yet it was anything but.

Dr. Richter had returned to Chastain Park just after dinner and stopped by briefly to assess Ruth. The knowledge of what he had done to his own mother and to so many other women made her skin crawl, but she carefully maintained her composure in his presence.

Shirley grabbed an envelope from a small stack under the bed and copied Robert's wording, word for word. Its purpose was clear enough…to avoid detection of escape for as long as possible.

Ruth was fast asleep, snoring loudly and oblivious to the world around her. There was not so much as a flinch when Shirley turned off her bedside lamp. The room fell into pitch blackness for a minute before slowly easing into slight transparency with the glow of the moonlight. She took a deep breath, held it, and let go. A feeling of nervousness hit her like a wave, and she sat on the cold floor, trying her best to stay focused. This was the only way. Once she left, there would be no choice but to follow through and make it to the other side. Failure would quickly translate to solitary confinement, and even working at Francis Hall would, undoubtedly, be prohibited. She would become her aunt Catherine, hopelessly bound to a lifetime of institutionalization.

Just enough light protruded from the windows to see the dresser. She slipped off her nightgown and into her day dress, hopeful that it was the last time she would ever don the horrible uniform. She would burn it, toss it into a bonfire, while taking a swig of whiskey in celebration of her freedom. She would never purchase a black dress again. From here on out, every dress she owned would be bright and cheerful.

Her only possession was the single letter her sorority sisters had sent months ago. "We wish you all the best and think of you every day. We cannot wait to see you when you are well. Enjoy the magazines, books, and desserts! Merry Christmas!" it read. She knew it like the back of her hand, and it served as a reminder that people still cared. For months now, she had held onto it like a security blanket. Her sorority sisters were her only hope of normalcy outside of the institution. But what if they had moved on, forgotten her, or worse, decided to distance themselves because of her mental state? She forced herself to not indulge the thought further and stuffed the letter safely into her pocket.

There was nothing to do but wait. The room vibrated with Ruth's snores…one deep, loud breath in, followed by a few seconds of perfect stillness, and then one deep sigh out. According to the clock above the doorway, each snore was perfectly spaced five seconds apart, with twelve per minute and seven hundred and twenty per hour. For the first hour, Shirley counted for fun, pleased to find that she could accurately tell time from Ruth's snores alone. The night grew darker and her eyelids heavy. A few times, she drifted off to sleep, scolding herself each time for not being on her guard. At exactly two o'clock, the soft jingle of keys came from the hall, and the door slowly crept open, no faster than a snail's pace, for fear of creating the dreaded creak that might give them away before they even had a chance to start. Robert's head appeared through the opening, and Shirley quietly got up from the bed, stuffing pillows beneath the sheets and leaving the letter beside as instructed. She stuffed Robert's detailed instructions into the pocket with the Christmas card and followed the dim light that streamed through the doorway, walking on tiptoe and carrying her shoes.

Just as they reached the door, they stopped in their tracks. There was an eerie silence in the absence of Ruth's snores. Had she awoken? What if she screamed? They waited and listened, and seconds later, the steady, comforting repetition of inhalations and exhalations resumed like the ebbing and flowing of waves. Both breathed a sigh of relief and quickly exited the room, Robert taking care to lock the door behind them.

The hallway was empty, devoid of the hustle found during the daytime. Two of the night-shift nurses slept in the nurses' station, and the pair slipped down the hall towards the stairwell. Despite their best efforts to exit quietly, the rusty, old door creaked open in a God-awful pitch, screaming their escape to anyone who might listen, but no one heard. Patients and staff alike were still recovering from the stomach bug that had ravaged the halls, whisked away into a dream-like escape of their own. They breathlessly ran towards the basement and through a second quieter door, expecting to be discovered at any minute and pleasantly surprised by the lack of rustling feet, alarm bells, and frantic voices. It was a small miracle that neither had time to appreciate in the moment.

The hall was dim, only lit by a lone bulb left on in the laundry room. Robert led the way towards the kitchen and past the double doors with the word 'Morgue' above. A cold chill ran down her spine as she thought of how many bodies had passed through those doors over the years. The holding cells, where Johnny MacIntyre and Walter Cummings had been held following that fateful Christmas dinner party, were no better. The stench of mildew and sewage permeated the air, and a rat scurried across the floor from one of the holding cells and towards the kitchen.

The kitchen was pitch black, and Robert flipped the switch by the door, casting fluorescent lighting throughout the room. It was tidy enough. Dinner plates from the night before had been washed and set out to dry. Five bags of potatoes sat along the floor and would be made into hashbrowns, French fries, potato bread, and mashed potatoes the following day. Robert began to open cabinets, searching for something. A hoard of canned and jarred goods and baking ingredients occupied most of the shelves. Below sat bags of flour, one of which was riddled with holes, its innards spilling around it like dusty snow. Finally, he found what he was looking for. He handed two candles to Shirley and kept two for himself, lighting them with a match. The round, red clock over the door read twenty past two. They still had nearly four hours until the majority of the hospital awoke for morning medications.

"You'll need these," he said in explanation.

Though Shirley wondered how they would get out and where they would go, she refrained from asking. She was going to trust him and would be able to question him later, after this was all over.

He led her out of the kitchen, shutting down the lights behind him. There was an unpleasantness about the hallway, as though someone might pop out of the shadows at any moment. The very real possibility that this could happen, that someone might still discover them, sent shivers down Shirley's spine. They passed the laundry room, its solitary light continuing to shine like a beacon of hope.

The morgue loomed ahead, separated only by a short stretch of lime-green walls, the paint of which peeled off in heavy chunks. Once closer, it became evident that there was a light on inside. It was dim, nearly unnoticeable unless looking directly at the doors, yet nonetheless, an undeniable illumination behind the crisscross etching of the rectangular windows that had not been there minutes before. They stood back, pressing their bodies against the wall, silent. Robert quickly blew out the four candles. Who was in there at this hour? Had a patient passed away and been brought down for keeping? If that was the case, why had they heard nothing? There had been no scampering of feet nor voices while they were in the kitchen. But perhaps there had been, and they had been too distracted to notice.

Another horrible rat, fattened off food in the kitchen and God-only-knows what else, scampered past Shirley's feet and towards the holding cells, and she threw her hand across her mouth to hold in a scream. Robert hardly seemed to notice the rat, instead staring ahead, wide-eyed, focused on something. She could see his lips silently mutter words which she could not distinguish. She followed his gaze, and a fear like none she had ever encountered shot through her body.

The room was full, filled with the fairly young and the fairly old and everything in between. They were pale, sickly looking, dead but very much alive, and stared back through the glass windows at Robert and Shirley, studying them with the intensity that one might study the dissection of a frog in science class. The presence of the duo was cause for great interest. Of the twenty or so faces, one stood out. Shirley quietly uttered the name that haunted her every thought yet was nearly too devastating to speak aloud…Barbara. And then Robert noticed someone equally implausible. She moved effortlessly through the closed double doors, the soft glow of her pale skin and white nurse's uniform offsetting the dimness of the light-starved hallway. A sad expression clung to the face of Margaret Baker. With the slowness of moving through pudding, she motioned for them to follow and then turned and walked down the hall, moving in perfect silence, not a breath nor footstep to be heard.

Neither moved. Whatever *it* was, both saw clearly. They could not deny what was happening, though it was impossible in every sense of the word. Ms. Baker had been dead for months now. Robert had even attended her funeral two-and-a-half hours east in her hometown of Reading. Was it truly the spirit of the sweet nurse who had been killed, here to provide help, or was it some deceptive ploy to ruin their escape? They were on a tight timeline, and following a ghost, or whatever it was, around was not part of the plan. Margaret turned back and motioned once more, her eyes wide and insistent, her sweet face stern, and Robert began to follow. Shirley reluctantly hung several feet behind, wishing he had not, but having no choice but to go along. Behind her, the ghosts of the morgue were crowding the hallway, staring, watching, glowing in the darkness. Barbara stood at the helm beside a little boy, a cigarette dangling from one hand, blowing clouds of ethereal smoke into the stale air, and in a moment of sheer irrationality, Shirley ran back.

"What are you doing?" Robert called out after her.

Shirley seemed to take no notice. The two women embraced. "I'm so sorry I couldn't save you," Shirley cried. "It's all my fault."

"You mustn't blame yourself for what happened. Promise me you won't." She took another drag of the cigarette, the tip of which glowed a bright red.

"I'll never forgive myself."

"Please," her eyes pleaded. "I'm okay now." She smiled down at John. "You must go now. Go!" she yelled in a voice so loudly that the hallway walls seemed to vibrate, and a renewed fear of waking those above flowed through her veins.

"Go now. Go!" the others repeated loudly, urgently. Shirley watched in terror as the faces began to morph and stretch unnaturally, resembling something out of a Salvador Dali painting, before disappearing entirely, leaving only the lingering scent of cigarette smoke behind.

Margaret stood across from the stairwell, and the heavy red door that was always kept locked slowly creaked open on its own accord. Robert had passed by the door numerous times before and never given it much thought, believing it to be a storage room or root cellar. It was dark inside. He lit the candles once again and shined the light into the room, which, when illuminated, revealed much more than a walled off chamber. It was a passageway.

"Follow the tunnel to the end. Take the branch towards the right. There you will find your freedom." Margaret smiled at the two one last time before disappearing before their eyes.

Tunnel? Neither were aware of a tunnel, other than the idle gossip Robert heard from older patients. Jack Eidson had mentioned a tunnel to him once as he helped him back into bed, describing how, in the old days, orderlies would transport him through a tunnel to Francis Hall for bingo. Robert had attributed his stories to failing memory, especially since none of the other staff members ever mentioned anything of it, and had almost forgotten about Jack's story entirely.

It was a tunnel, indeed. He could not see beyond fifteen feet or so, but it appeared to go on quite a ways. Cobwebs clung to the ceiling, and he suddenly understood the entry source of the hospital's basement rats. The floor was made of thick, non-slip rubber, and as they walked, they could see that the walls had been painted, likely decades before, with amateur pictures of flowery fields and sunny skies, likely to create some pleasantry along the walkway.

Robert ran back to the heavy metal door and closed it behind them, masking their escape as quietly as possible, and the two forged ahead into darkness. Shirley wondered why the tunnel was no longer used and why had it been kept such a secret. Maybe it was viewed as a safety threat. Depending on where it terminated, it could easily aid patients who wanted to escape.

A lightbulb with a pull string hung over them, and much to their surprise, still worked, casting light far behind and ahead. The light flickered for a moment, threatening to cast them back into darkness, but then, as if deciding against such cruelty, steadied. They stopped to catch their breath, and Shirley slipped on the shoes she had been carrying, relieved to no longer have to worry about the sound of footsteps setting off alarms. As much as they wanted to use the overhead light to guide them, they knew it would leave a trail, and Robert pulled the string, once again returning them to candlelight.

They walked slowly, trying to avoid walking into walls as the tunnel twisted this way and that. The drawings on the walls dwindled after a bit, revealing a long stretch of bland yellow.

Finally, Shirley gathered up the courage to ask, "Do you know where this is going? Is this part of the plan?" If she hoped he would say yes, not to worry, that he had been through the tunnel several times and knew exactly where they were going, she was sorely mistaken. Robert shook his head. The plan had been to return to the first floor and exit out of the pool room door, which contained a simple lock easy enough for picking. Surely, there would have been footprints left in the snow behind them, but by then, they would have been long gone. It was a fair escape plan, the only one he had been able to finagle with such short notice. He had not even known the tunnel truly existed until now, but if it led to where he thought it would, they might just end up exactly where they needed to be, minus a trail, other than a few drops of candle wax. It was brilliant.

"It is better. Much better." He seemed suddenly enthusiastic.

A fork in the tunnel appeared, just as Margaret had promised. A metal sign reading 'Francis Hall' pointed left, while a similar sign with a picture of railroad tracks pointed right. The two set off in the direction of the latter, and Shirley noticed a pep in Robert's step as he led the way. She assumed that this is what he had meant when he said better…a path directly to the railroads, one that would almost certainly guarantee a successful escape.

After walking a half mile underground, the tunnel terminated with another heavy, red door, exactly like the one near the morgue. It was locked, but after a few minutes of picking it with his tools, it opened. A rush of cold wind hit their faces. They ascended a small set of concrete stairs and emerged at the edge of the farm fields. Soon enough, they would be filled with eligible patients, planting the next round of crops for the summer and fall. But for now, the land sat waiting beneath a thick layer of snow, taking its final rest before the growing season. Train tracks lied just beyond the fields, and Shirley and Robert walked alongside, waiting and shivering in the cold.

"Is there a train coming?" she asked after a while.

Robert glanced at his watch. "Yes, but we're here a little earlier than expected. It's three twenty-five. The train does not arrive until three forty."

A tree had fallen along the wood line. Robert brushed off the snow, and the two sat and waited, huddled together, their shared body heat keeping each other warm. A couple of snow rabbits bounced merrily around, this way and that, fattened up for the winter. A lone owl hoot-hooted in the distance. Moonlight bounced off the snow, creating a daylight effect that negated any need for candles.

Eventually, a light appeared in the distance, shining through the trees like a rising sun and casting shadows behind them. The rumble on the tracks was loud, though it moved slowly, cautiously, down the icy tracks. Several passenger cars sat behind the engine, followed by two or three stock cars.

"We're going to hop aboard with the livestock," he said, pointing towards the back of the train. "When I say go, I want you to run as fast as you can!" He was yelling now. The train was growing louder and louder. "I will jump on first and then help you up."

They watched the passing of the finely-painted passenger cars, and as the rusted livestock cars grew nearer, Robert yelled, "Go!" He sprinted alongside the train, Shirley close behind, and jumped aboard the first of the livestock cars. He slid the door open and reached his arm out, grabbing Shirley and pulling her up and into the car beside him. There were several sheep, all sleeping, except for one that eyed them suspiciously. Robert slid the car door closed. Shirley did not want to see the hospital ever again but could not help but watch it slide by, out of her life forever. How much she had changed during the three months within its walls. Her time there had taken a part of her soul and left her with the lesson that evil really does exist, sometimes in the places least expected. As she stared out deep in thought, a bright light suddenly caught her eye. At first, she thought it was a couple of flashlights, perhaps a mob of angry staff forming a search party after realizing that she was not in her room. But the light was not coming from outside. A new horror came over her as she realized that it was *inside*, flashing brightly behind the hospital windows, jumping wildly about and spreading down the building. An entire hall of windows glowed an eerie orange and yellow.

"Look!" she demanded. Robert stared at the hospital, trying to comprehend the terrible sight before him.

"What is that?" he asked, baffled.

"I think it's on fire!" Shirley shrieked. "We must go back."

Robert watched for a moment before responding coldly, "There's nothing we can do." His apparent lack of empathy could not have been more shocking.

"They're still asleep and locked in their rooms. We can't leave them there," she pleaded.

Robert looked at Shirley sternly. He needed for her to understand. "Say we jump off the train and run back lickety-split. By the time we got there, the whole thing would be a giant inferno. It would be too late to save anyone. We would become arson suspects and probably end up imprisoned for life." He struggled to maintain his composure as he spoke, and Shirley could see now that he did care. "If we stay here, it will just be assumed that we died in the fire, too. No one will come looking for us. Don't you see? We have to keep going."

A minute later, the hospital was out of sight. Both hoped they were mistaken, that the light in the windows was an odd reflection of moonlight and nothing more, but deep down, they knew. They sat in silence for several hours as the train sped through long stretches of farmland and mountains, slowing but not stopping as it passed by empty train stations, and then speeding back up again. The sheep that had eyed them suspiciously when they boarded had fallen asleep with the others. The train moved through a small town, slowing as it approached a station, and Robert nudged Shirley awake.

"We've got to jump off now." Shirley followed him to the door, and when he pulled it open, she could see the edge of the morning sun sitting on the horizon. It felt warmer, and there was no snow on the ground. The two jumped off, right after another, down into the dirt. Shirley dusted off her arms and dress.

"Where are we?"

"A little town in West Virginia called Summersville. My grandmother used to live out here and left her house to me when she died. It's been mostly abandoned since she passed, but it's in good enough shape."

By the time they had finally walked the three miles to the house, the sun had risen, and the first batch of early birds were hopping into their cars and heading off to work. Her feet ached in the stiff leather shoes, and she eagerly tossed them onto the floor as soon as they walked through the front door. Her body collapsed onto a chair, where she sat for a time and prayed for those patients left behind. The question of how the fire began nagged at her and made her question whether they, in their hurry to leave, had perhaps forgotten a candle, though Robert still had the four in his pocket, having carried them the entire trip to Summersville to avoid leaving behind a trail.

The house was a small, cottage-like structure with three bedrooms, one bathroom, and a large room that served as both a living room and kitchen. It was cozy albeit a bit old-fashioned, and were it not for the thick layer of dust that covered everything like a fine snow, the house could have easily passed for being occupied. It had been wallpapered in early-century, faded-pink floral patterns, with trim and doors painted in a sage green and windows covered in white lace. The sofa and chairs were upholstered in blue velvet, and each of the beds sat beneath handmade quilts. Once Robert returned with groceries and the smell of eggs and bacon permeated the air, it began to feel like home.

The neighbors sat fairly dispersed with several acres between them and hardly noticed that life had returned to the Patterson residence. When a neighbor from down the road finally did come to check in, Robert merely explained that he and his new bride had moved in, opting for a life away from the city. The story satisfied any curiosity adequately, and no one seemed to question it. It was the truth, at least part of it. She and Robert had married days later in a quiet ceremony with only a priest present, barely having become acquainted but already knowing each other entirely.

A week after moving in, Shirley came across a newspaper article in the *Charleston Daily Times* entitled *Catastrophic Fire Ravages Mental Institution Leaving Only Four Survivors*.

In the early morning hours of Saturday, March 20th, a fire broke out at Chastain Park Psychiatric Hospital, a renowned Pennsylvania mental health facility. Although circumstances surrounding the fire remain unclear, investigators suspect it to have originated in the basement. A total of ninety-two bodies of patients and staff have been found, with most now identified. Two remain missing, and there are four survivors. The surviving patients, all males, have been taken to a local hospital for treatment of minor burns and smoke inhalation. Though their escape details are unknown at this time, none are suspected of any wrongdoing due to the severity of their handicaps.

We spoke with local residents who were horrified by what took place within walking distance of their homes. Jeffrey Webber lives across the street from the facility and told us that Friday evening into Saturday morning was just like any other. He and his wife spent Saturday helping to search for victims and were horrified by the destruction inside.

"It was a mess. It looked like someone had torched the whole hospital and then…"

"Robert, look at this! How awful," Shirley lamented as she handed the paper across the table to Robert. They were finishing up breakfast and coffee before Robert left for work. He had recently gotten a job at a local grocer. No one questioned his past or the alias he used, only whether he was capable of stocking shelves and taking inventory. It paid the bills for the time being, and he actually found himself enjoying his work.

"Terrible, just terrible." Robert had lost several of his favorite patients. The article mentioned several names that stung particularly hard, including Johnny MacIntyre, the twenty-year-old epileptic who had shared in their Christmas celebration and spent a night in confinement as punishment; Peter Blakely, a forty-two-year-old who had been born with severe mental delays; Buck Thompson, institutionalized since the age of five due to frequent seizures, who, a week prior to the fire, had celebrated his twenty-second birthday; and Johnny Moreland, a thirty-one-year-old brain injury survivor who possessed the most heart-warming smile. The fact that there was no way to save them or to have prevented what happened tore apart his heart, and when he was alone, he mourned the lives they had been robbed of and what should have been. Some days, though, he wondered whether these men were better off.

Not long after settling in, people around town began to refer to the newbies as the Clarks. The wife, Betty, was sweet enough and a great gardener, very willing to share her surplus cucumbers and peas, and Gerald, her husband, was handy and helpful to any neighbor in need. Everyone just assumed those were their names anyway because those were the names the couple used. Shirley dyed her hair a honey blonde, and Robert adopted a top hat and glasses as part of his wardrobe. They had mutually decided it best to play it safe the first few years to see how things played out in the aftermath of the fire. There was always a fear in the back of their minds that they would be held responsible if it was discovered that they survived. It was for this very reason that Shirley made the difficult decision to abandon the estate left to her by her late parents, as well as her degree. If she remained presumed dead, she could start over, free from judgment for having been institutionalized and free from the risk of being found guilty of deaths she did not cause. So, out of fear, she let her past slip away.

Shortly after moving in, the Clarks burned any relics of their past…driver's licenses, clothes, hospital bands and badges, the instructions left under the door by Robert, and the Christmas card the sorority had sent. Shirley did not even have a single picture of her parents to remember them by, though Robert promised to purchase what he could when her parent's estate went up for auction. Several months later, he did just that and returned with Janet Fitzpatrick's silver serving set, jewelry, and bakeware and several pieces of Bill Fitzpatrick's handmade, intricately-carved furniture, along with several photo albums and family cookbooks. After his own mother passed away, Robert similarly neglected his own inheritance, obtaining only a few sentimental items later at auction.

They met a man in town who created new driver's licenses with the names Elizabeth and Gerald Clark and birthdates a few years off from their actual. He even created passports, birth certificates, and college diplomas, though Betty declined a diploma. Her dreams had changed, and her heart was now in the home. They paid him handsomely for his efforts, and he, the respectable man he was, never told a soul of the work he did. It was a secret that even his wife would neglect to discover.

Betty and Gerald tried desperately for a family but found themselves unable to conceive a child, yet they were anything but childless. Over the years, they would take in many children in need, and they became known in Summersville as an orphanage of sorts, though Betty hated the term because it sounded too institutional. Some children were young toddlers, others teenagers, and at one point, they housed eight children at once. Many came to love them for the role they played in their lives when they needed someone the most. Their house was noisy, messy, even chaotic at times, but it was perfect. The elusive happiness Shirley once thought impossible had at long last been captured, not in career and social status, but in home and family.

Chapter Thirteen

With great trepidation, a doctor with silver, balding hair pulled back into a low ponytail conducted a physical examination on his new patient. His hand shook as he wrote in the medical record, his eyes unwavering from the woman before him. His handwriting resembled that of a young elementary school student rather than a professional. Two female nurses stood on either side of him, curiously watching the patient as one might watch a black widow, intrigued yet defensively prepared. At last, when the physician had jotted down a few more scribbles, they left the room and locked the door securely behind them, though, in reality, the lock did little to calm their fears. A police officer stood on either side of the door and greeted the physician with a nod.

Once back at the nurses' station, the trio spoke in hushed tones about the older woman who had arrived the morning prior. She had been found wandering along train tracks in the middle of the night and not adequately dressed for the cold.

"Ms. Catherine Holly was admitted just after seven yesterday morning, brought in by local police for treatment of burns to her upper extremities, accompanied by possible altered mental status. Patient is well known to Huckleford Medical Center and suffers from schizophrenia, delusions of grandeur, dissociative personality disorder, and suicidal/homicidal ideations. She was formerly institutionalized at Chastain Park Psychiatric Hospital, which, as I'm sure you've heard by now, has been lost to arson. Patient's wounds are being treated with a combination of topical vitamin C and zinc oxide. A prophylactic Penicillin regimen was ordered, which I understand she refuses, believing the pills to be poisoned. Patient does not recall the fire nor leaving the scene." The doctor cleared his throat. "But it is suspected that she initiated the fire, which has killed all but four of the hospital's residents and staff. I urge you ladies to exercise extreme precautions with all interactions."

"Yes, Dr. Philips. Of course. I have reviewed the records and understand that the patient has several…aliases?" The nurse was young but one of the brightest and had been specifically chosen to handle this case because of her success with some of the hospital's most difficult psychiatric patients.

"That is correct." He looked through the record. "The patient often refers to herself as Shirley Fitzpatrick, which I believe is actually the name of her niece, if I'm not mistaken. When she assumes the role of Shirley, she believes that she is a young woman being unjustly held following the deaths of her parents in an air disaster. She also believes that medical staff are attempting to poison her via gassing and the injection of hallucinogenic agents and, therefore, has a habit of foregoing her medical treatment, leading to further psychiatric decline.

Ms. Holly sometimes assumes the identity of Betty Clark, an out-of-town resident who famously escaped a house fire as a child. I believe the real Betty Clark currently resides in Summersville, West Virginia, which the patient often refers to as her own home. When she adopts this personality, she becomes very affectionate towards children and gentlemen and has been known to kiss an unsuspecting male nurse or two, which is why I insist upon female nurses and shifts in pairs. Because of the severity of the allegations against her, police will remain stationed outside of her door at all times. Again, you must not let your guard down."

Betty sat in front of the mirror and twirled her long, gray locks between her fingers. Perhaps she would braid it today. Gerald always liked it that way. She stared wearily across the bathroom and watched as a small ladybug climbed down the wall. Her garden was full of the tiny creatures this year due to the aphids, and one had finally found its way into the house. The ladybug crawled onto some roses, which sat in a vase by the sink, and settled on a leaf. She would leave it be for now. It did not bother her and actually looked quite sweet amongst the flowers. She rubbed some Vaseline over her wrinkled skin, giving her face an instant glow, before swiping on a few strokes of mascara. Today was a special day. Amanda was coming.

Decades ago, when she was a little girl, Betty and Gerald had fostered her over a two-year period, and as an adult, she never wasted an opportunity to show her gratitude. She had the habit of visiting every now and then, always with groceries and toiletries in tow, and had a cheery demeanor that was contagious.

If only her arms were not giving her such trouble, today of all days. She lifted a bandage and looked down at the red, blistering welts that occupied both limbs and scolded herself for being so careless. The day before, she had been poking at the embers in the fireplace when a frail log disintegrated, sending sparks this way and that and onto the long sleeves of her fleece nightgown. She had immediately flung it off, but both arms had already sustained mild burns. A doctor in town had bandaged the wounds up nicely and given her special ointments to use, but the pain was enough to drive her crazy.

Despite the minor inconvenience of not feeling her best, the home was clean, coffee was brewing, and a loaf of coffee cake was nearly ready to come out of the oven. It was eight forty-five, and Amanda was not due until nine. Betty sat down in the floral-stitched lounge chair. Another ladybug had made its way into the den and was inching ever so slowly across the ceiling and towards the large bay window that overlooked the garden. She opened the window a crack and then returned to the comfort of the chair. Her fingers divided her hair and wove it into a braid that traversed the back of her head and terminated on one side in a red ribbon. At last, there was a knock, and the front door opened.

"Good morning," came a joyful voice from behind her. A slightly overweight woman in her mid-fifties emerged wearing jeans and a yellow T-shirt and sporting a friendly smile. She wore her brown hair pulled back into a bun. Her face was gentle, and there was a kindness behind her eyes. While Betty had remained close with all of the former foster children, Amanda was her favorite.

"Mandy, how wonderful! Come in, dear." And then, seeing the groceries in her arms, "Oh, you can set those on the counter. I had a little accident," she said, lifting up her arms and revealing the bandages. "Nothing to worry about."

"Goodness, what happened?" Amanda rushed to set down the groceries and then to Betty's side.

"Oh, you know how it is when you get older. I was just fixing the fire and kept my arm a little too close for a little too long and…"

"You need to see a doctor," Amanda said, lifting the bandages. "These look horrible."

"I've already seen one, and I've got a special cream for it. The doctor said it might take a few days before it feels better. But really, it's nothing to get worked up over. How was the drive?"

On the weekends, it was a half-hour drive, but during rush-hour traffic, it was easily double.

"There was a lot of traffic just outside of town. Car accident at the light. It didn't look bad when I drove past it, but Remmington was backed up for miles."

"I've been telling Gerald that someone was going to get hurt up there. Folks are always running that light."

"Where is Gerald?"

"He's at the hardware store picking up a part for his tractor. Gas leak, I think. He should be home any minute."

The oven beeped, and the coffee cake came out looking just like the picture in the cookbook. The sides had a nice crispness to the edges, courtesy of loads of butter and sugar, and a sweet smell permeated the air. The women sat down to enjoy the cake with coffee and discussed Amanda's work at the post office and her plans for retirement the following year. She had already cut back her hours to thirty-two per week since injuring her ankle on the job two months prior. Suddenly, Betty let out a horrible, blood-curdling shriek that nearly made Amanda jump out of her chair.

"What…what is it?" she asked.

Betty stared at the floor, watching something move this way and that, around Amanda's feet and then towards the kitchen. Amanda followed her gaze but could not see whatever it was that commanded Betty's attention.

"A snake!" Betty yelled.

"A snake?" This time, Amanda jumped out of her seat. She had heard on the news that copperheads were particularly invasive that summer and carefully inched her way to the broom closet, not taking her eyes off the floor. Another scream came from the den. "Where is it?" Amanda yelled frantically, grabbing the broom.

"Over there by the television. Be careful!" she cautioned through clenched teeth. "Ooh, there's another by the sofa…and two by the chair!"

"I don't see them!" Amanda scoured the room, looking for the slightest of movement along the carpet and under furniture, but there was nothing, not a slither to be seen nor a hiss to be heard.

"By your feet!"

"What?" Amanda jumped again and, when she realized there was no snake, took a seat on the sofa. "I don't see anything, Betty. Are you sure there are snakes?"

"Of course, I'm sure," Betty retorted, somewhat annoyed. As if she would make up something like that. And she most certainly did not have dementia like poor Ms. Abagail down the street. That poor woman had to have hired help day and night just to ensure she ate and used the bathroom.

The front door opened, and Gerald emerged, carrying a red gas container and a bag of tools. He set them down. Over the years, his blonde hair had faded to a soft, silvery white, though his face had aged very little, save for a few laugh lines. He wore a plaid shirt and work pants and smelled like an auto repair shop.

"Morning, Mandy." He lifted a hand in greeting. When he saw the broom and the fear in the women's eyes, he grew concerned. "Is everything alright?"

"It's those darn snakes. They were in the house again, but they must have just gone back out," Betty said, pointing to the window she had opened earlier.

"I'll have a look around and see what I can see," Gerald offered, a lack of urgency in his voice. He grabbed a soda from the fridge before walking out the back.

"If you're getting snakes, you need to call an exterminator. You can't be living with those things coming inside. Some of those'll kill you."

"We just had a pest control company come out for spiders. If it's not one thing, it's another," she nervously laughed.

"Well, I hope you can get rid of them, but it might be hard, living near a creek."

Betty closed the window. The two women sat back down to finish their coffee, and after a half hour, the incident had nearly been forgotten. Amanda had an appointment and had to leave but made Betty promise her that if the snakes returned, she and Gerald would come stay with her until it was taken care of. Betty agreed, though she knew that if she kept her word, they would become Amanda's houseguests at least once per week, which was just not a feasible possibility. She could not bring herself to share that they had already had an exterminator out twice for the snakes, yet no problem was ever found.

That evening, as she lied in bed, she felt completely and utterly sad. She struggled to hide her tears from Gerald, afraid that he would question what was wrong and she would not be able to tell him. Yet something nagged at her, dug a knife into her heart and twisted, as if someone she loved dearly had died, though the feelings made no sense at all. It's just part of getting older, she told herself and closed her eyes for the night. Tomorrow was another day.

Dr. Philips made his morning rounds, procrastinating and delaying the inevitable visit to the room of Ms. Catherine Holly. He could barely stand to look at her, knowing that she caused the deaths of his former colleague and personal friend, Dr. Carl Richter, and so many others. He would attend the doctor's funeral the following day, and several other funerals would fall the day after. Local morticians were so inundated with the dead that extras from Pittsburg and Philadelphia had traveled in to assist. Nonetheless, there was a job that needed to be done before he could continue with his day, and he reluctantly unlocked the door to her room.

Catherine was still in her nightgown. She wore her long silver hair in a braid, tied off neatly with a red ribbon, and looked like any grandmother one might see at the store or at a grandchild's school play. She pleasantly welcomed the doctor and his two nurses with a "Good morning." They responded in kind, and Dr. Philips wasted no time in removing the bandages and examining the burn wounds. The wounds appeared to be healing well. They showed signs of granulation, and dead skin was in the process of sloughing, revealing a pink, healthy layer beneath. Physically, she would be ready to discharge to a new asylum within a few days, but the problem lied with securing a facility willing to accept her. By now, everyone in the nation knew the name Catherine Holly, and no one wanted to touch her with a ten-foot pole. She was poison, and even uttering her name was venomous.

Because of the severity of the accusations against her, Ms. Holly had been placed on suicide watch and provided a twenty-four-hour, seven-day-a-week sitter, who rotated on an eight-hour schedule and could quickly alert staff should she try to climb out a window or hang herself from a bedsheet. The first-shift sitter was a middle-aged woman by the name of Martha Freemon, who had quickly become Catherine's sitter of choice. She wore her dark hair pulled back in a ponytail, and her dark skin carried a youthful glow. Catherine enjoyed talking to her. She felt as though she could trust her. Out of the many people who cared for the old woman, Martha was the only one who was not afraid of her. The hospital had given fair warning of the allegations against Ms. Holly and even offered to supply a second sitter during her shifts, but she had gladly accepted the job anyway, mostly out of curiosity, eager to get to know the woman who had burned down the old mental hospital. And she had not been disappointed. Martha watched as the doctor completed his examination, ever-so-slightly amused by his fear of Ms. Holly, though she would never admit it to anyone. She watched curiously as the trio left the room, locking in her and Catherine behind them, wondering what they would discuss out of earshot.

Once in the nurses' station, the doctor breathed a sigh of relief. The group sat in swivel chairs, and Dr. Philips scribbled a few final notes in the chart.

"I understand Ms. Holly continues to refuse Penicillin…and also Thorazine?" Dr. Philips inquired, looking at the nurses.

"Yes," one of the nurses answered. "As I fluffed her pillow this morning, I discovered a small collection of pills hidden underneath."

"It's no wonder she made such little progress at Chastain Park. Any attempt at controlling psychosis and delusions has been thwarted by her paranoia. I'd like to speak with the pharmacist and transition her oral medications to injections."

"Yes, of course."

"Dr. Philips," the other nurse chimed in. "I spoke with the sitter a few hours ago, and she sort of let it slip that Ms. Holly has claimed to see snakes crawling around the room. I think she only told me about it because she was just as worried as Ms. Holly about reptilian visitors, though obviously, there are none. Perhaps she could use some tips on how to handle Ms. Holly's hallucinations until the Thorazine takes effect?"

"Yes, of course. Sara, Ann, thank you for your input. I would like to have a word with the sitter. Would you send her out while you stay with Ms. Holly in the interim?"

"Yes, doctor."

A moment later, Martha emerged, and Dr. Philips motioned for her to sit down in the nurses' station.

"Hello again. Ms. Freemon, is it?"

"Yes."

"I'd like to ask a few questions about your interactions with Ms. Holly. Would you mind telling me a bit about how things are going?"

"Well, pretty normal for the most part. Ms. Holly talks quite a bit about how much she enjoys gardening and sometimes talks about her husband, Gerald. It seems like she's a happily married woman. She did complain of seeing snakes yesterday. I did not see any myself, though I will admit when the sun sets, the shadows from the tree outside the window can look like snakes if one's eyesight is not the best."

"How has her mood been?" the doctor asked, scribbling a few notes in the chart.

"I'd say it varies. She's pleasant enough to me." Martha ran her hand up her cheek, where it stayed for a moment, as if she was in deep thought. "But last night, I heard her crying, and when I asked her whether there was anything she wanted to talk about, she looked confused…seemed to have no idea why I would ask her that. So, I just let it go, and she seemed perfectly normal when she woke up."

"Has she mentioned anything about the fire or why she started it?"

"No, not that I can recall anyway."

"Thank you. Would you send the nurses back out?"

A moment later, the women rejoined him.

"I've been informed that Ms. Holly has family visiting this morning. Would you be so kind as to get her ready? They should arrive within the hour."

It was just before ten when Bill and Janet Fitzpatrick arrived at the hospital. They had argued on the drive over whether or not they should bother visiting, yet Janet had insisted upon it. She was as disgusted as everyone else by the awful act committed by her own flesh and blood, but it was her only sister. Life for her had been difficult, and despite her wrongdoings, she needed family.

"Um, excuse me. We're here to see Catherine Holly," said Bill to a woman at the front desk.

"Yes, we've been expecting you. Please, take a seat."

They waited a few minutes before being patted down by a security guard to search for any potential weapons. The contents of Janet's purse were tossed about, and a small pair of scissors was placed to the side. When it was clear that neither posed a safety threat nor intended to supply Ms. Holly with any potential hazards, they were escorted up to the fifth floor of wing C.

Two police officers stood stationed outside the door. Inside, Catherine and Martha sat on the bed, busily playing a game of checkers. Catherine looked up for a moment and then back down at the red and black board. Her teeth clenched, and a surge of fear ran through her veins. She would ignore the hallucinations. She would pretend that the visitors she recognized as her deceased parents were not there.

"Oh, Cat," Janet said, sitting down beside her, one arm laid sympathetically on her shoulder. "How are you?" She swallowed hard when she saw the bandaged arms, the reality of what her own flesh and blood had done suddenly making her queasy. How someone close to her had done something so horrendous would never make sense.

She watched as Catherine moved a checker piece past Martha's. "King me," she ordered gleefully, clapping her hands in celebration. It was as though no one besides her and Martha were there.

"Cat," Janet repeated. Catherine ignored the attempt at conversation and moved another piece closer to kingship. Janet was growing upset by her lack of acknowledgment, and Bill's facial expression seemed to convey, 'I told you so.' She had gone through considerable effort to make the visit, especially given recent events, and felt slighted.

Martha watched in quiet amusement at the drama playing out before her. It was just enough action to break up the monotony of the day and to keep her coming back. You never knew what you were going to get with Catherine Holly.

"Now, Ms. Holly, you've got visitors here to see you, and you haven't given them the time of day," Martha chimed in. "What's gotten into you?"

"It's Janet, your sister…and Bill. We're here to visit you." Her eyes pleaded with Catherine for some sort of acceptance of their mere presence, but Catherine was too busy plotting her next move.

"Martha, king me again," she commanded.

"Ms. Holly, may I have a word with you?" Martha asked. The visitors left the room for a moment while Martha confronted the issue head-on. "Now, your sister and her husband came a long way to see you. Why are you being so rude?"

"I have no sister," she said calmly, devoid of any emotion. "Do you see them, too?"

"See who? Those two?" she pointed at the door. "Of course I see them."

"They're not real, you know."

"What do you mean, not real? I saw them two with my own eyes."

"They're ghosts or hallucinations…I'm not sure which…of my mother and father, who died in that plane crash last year. They certainly aren't…real, and it's best if you just ignore them."

Martha did not know what to make of what she was hearing. But she knew she was not seeing ghosts or hallucinations. "Plane crash?" She could not recall any at all in recent years, not since the accident in London back in 1950. Heavy fog or something. "Just talk to them for a few minutes. Then I'm sure they'll be on their way. Can you do that for me?" she asked, giving Catherine a smile.

"You really think they're real?" Catherine asked again, struggling to comprehend.

"Yes," Martha assured her. "They're as real as you and me."

Faint voices seeped from the other side of the door. "I told you this wasn't a good idea. She's clearly too unstable for visitors. This isn't safe." "She's been through trauma herself, you know. We knew this was going to be difficult." "We should have come another time then." "But she needs us now!"

A few minutes later, the couple reentered, this time standing across the room. It was clear from their eavesdropping that Bill was more than eager to end the visit, but Janet had coerced him into staying a little longer. What happened next would make Janet regret ever having walked back through that door.

"How are you holding up?" Janet began.

"Alright, I guess," Catherine answered shortly.

"Does it hurt?" Janet asked, gently holding one of the bandaged arms.

"Some." She pulled her arm back, not wanting to get any closer to the woman whose face she had seen take on monstrous qualities not so long ago. She was afraid of her and hoped that would be enough conversation to satisfy whatever reason was concocted to visit.

But Janet had much more to talk about. For her, it was the perfect opportunity to discuss their childhood before things went horribly wrong and all of the memories of old. Catherine listened, not saying much. "Bill, you wouldn't believe it. This one time, Catherine and I were in the neighbor's yard, stealing some strawberries to surprise Mother with, and his dog came rambling out after us. I lost my strawberries running, but Catherine would not give in. She fought that dog off with her bare hands until it relented. Keep in mind, she was only a ten-year-old girl!"

"Why do you keep calling me Catherine? That's not my name. And how could I possibly remember such a thing when I wasn't even born yet? You're my mother, not my sister."

Martha continued to watch, unable to take her eyes off of the mysterious family. It was better than any soap opera she had watched. Take that back. It was better than any drama in her own life, and she had a lot of it. Only a bowl of buttery popcorn could have made it better.

Neither Janet nor Bill knew what to say. They stared, listening, trying to comprehend what was being said to them. Did she really think they were her parents? How long had *that* been going on, and why had they not been warned by the hospital?

"Catherine," Bill began, "are you alright?"

"Shirley," Catherine corrected, laughing in amusement at their mistake. "I'm Shirley. You just called me Catherine, too."

Martha laughed, too and caught herself, quickly turning her chuckle into a cough before anyone else noticed.

"No, Shirley is off at school. She wanted to come, but…" Janet said, confused.

Her face grew red, and her fists clinched up again. She wanted to throw something. Why were they doing this to her? Why were they teasing her like this?

"Mother, I *am* Shirley!" she yelled at the top of her lungs, "your daughter!"

"Cat, please stop it," Janet begged, wondering if her response was part of some elaborate joke. "That's enough."

And before anyone could stop her, she lunged at Janet, pinning her against the floor. Martha rushed to grab the officers, who worked to remove Janet from her grasp and restrain Catherine, who had taken on an almost unnatural strength.

"Get her away from me! Get her away!" Janet yelled.

At last, the officers pried her free and then quickly escorted Bill and Janet out of the room. It would be the last time Catherine ever saw Janet as Bill forbade any future visits, fearing for his wife's safety.

But Martha was not deterred. She continued to sit daily, lured in by the drama and infamy of her patient, while the hospital desperately attempted to find a long-term psychiatric solution for Catherine Holly. One day, as the women sat on the bed, playing a game of bridge, Catherine's cheery demeanor became unexpectedly solemn.

"I didn't mean to kill them all, you know. It was an accident."

Martha nearly dropped the coffee she was sipping. Up until this point, she had admitted nothing to anyone, and the case against her was held up only by circumstantial evidence that could easily enough be dismissed in the court of law.

"What do you mean?" she asked, wondering whether it was a misunderstanding.

"I only meant to kill Dr. Richter and his nurse Cynthia. They were horrible, awful people who tried to poison me and held me there against my will. I planned to taint their food using chemicals from the morgue, so one night, I escaped my room and made it down there. I lit a candle to avoid having to turn on bright lights, and as I was gathering what I needed, I accidentally knocked the candle over. First, some white linens on a gurney caught fire, and the next thing I knew, the wall was ablaze. I tried spraying it with water from the sink, but it was already too big. The whole place became a giant inferno in a matter of minutes. I didn't know what to do, so I ran. I ran through some old tunnels, out to the train tracks, where I walked until dawn, when some folks found me. It was an accident, no matter what they say. But I'm glad they're all dead." Catherine uttered the last words with pleasure, and Martha stared back in disbelief.

Catherine's eyes had grown wide, and a large smile spanned her face, revealing teeth badly in need of dental repair. A sickening laugh erupted from within. That was the last straw for Martha. When her eight-hour shift came to an end, so too did her relationship with Ms. Holly. She would not come back ever again, for something in that laugh had shaken her to the core. It was raw, frightening, and evil. She had taken a brush with the insane a little too far, and she knew it, and now it was time to distance herself.

Catherine was eventually moved to the John Fowler Sanitorium, where she continued to live out the remainder of her life as Shirley, Betty, and, very occasionally, Catherine. Charges against her were quickly dismissed as she was found mentally unfit to stand trial. The daughter of Janet and Bill would maintain visits from time to time. In fact, Shirley became the sole visitor of the old woman, visiting on birthdays and holidays and always against the wishes of her parents. But years later, the visits abruptly ceased after Catherine attempted to strangle a six-month-pregnant Shirley, causing her to nearly lose her child.

The burnt-out shell of the old Chastain Park Psychiatric Hospital continues to stand, luring in the young and naïve for a chance to walk the halls of the notorious asylum. Many claim to see a mysterious boy in the attic. Others have seen the dead roam as if they are living, either unaware that they have died or unwilling to move on.

The lucky ones make it out unscathed. But every now and then, there is a certain waywardness that takes over the property that sparks an electrical charge in the air and an innate fear deep within. When this happens, the evil of Chastain Park abounds, hungry for new victims, seeking to destine visitors to their own psychiatric demise…or to never escape at all.

Medication Key

Medication	Side Effect
White pill	Placebo
Gray pill	Placebo
Brown tablets	Placebo
Green capsule	Hallucinations of Regina
Blue pill	Hallucinations of snakes
Pink pill	Hallucinations of children in the attic
Yellow pill	Paranoia, fear of being poisoned
Red tablet	Hallucinations of a deceased Janet Fitzpatrick/monster

About the Author

Anita Giannantonio is a Pennsylvania-based horror novelist whose passion for spine-chilling stories began with a lifelong fascination with horror films and books, further fueled by her own paranormal encounters. Her novels masterfully dive into the timeless battle between good and evil, gripping readers with tension and eerie suspense. Notably, each of her novels is crafted with precisely thirteen chapters—a nod to the superstition that led hotels and apartment buildings to omit the thirteenth floor. She lives with her husband and their five children, finding inspiration in both family life and the mysteries lurking beyond the ordinary.